Gwendo... ... part of S.... London for which she still has a tremendous affection. She was educated at one of the Haberdasher's Schools and then read History at Lady Margaret Hall, Oxford. After a short period doing research and teaching, she married, and it was while her husband was Professor of Mediaeval History in the University of St Andrews that she first began writing crime fiction.

In the early 1970s she returned to live near London when her husband, Dr Lionel Butler, became Principal of The Royal Holloway College, University of London. She is now a widow and lives in Surrey; she has one daughter.

Gwendoline Butler spends her time travelling, and looking at pictures, furniture and buildings. She has also found time to publish some thirty-odd books – she says she has always been too alarmed to count the exact number.

by the same author

A Coffin for the Canary
A Coffin for Pandora
A Coffin from the Past
Coffin Waiting
Coffin Following
A Nameless Coffin
Coffin in Malta
Coffin for Baby
Coffin in Oxford
Make Me a Murderer
Death Lives Next Door
The Interloper
The Dull Dead
The Murdering Kind
Dead in a Row
Receipt for Murder
Coffin on the Water
Coffin in Fashion

GWENDOLINE BUTLER

Coffin's
Dark Number

FONTANA/Collins

First published by Geoffrey Bles Ltd 1969
First issued in Fontana Paperbacks 1989

Copyright © Gwendoline Butler 1969

Made and printed in Great Britain by
William Collins Sons & Co. Ltd, Glasgow

There were three tapes, running about twenty-five minutes each, but Coffin played them for hours and hours. Over and over again. He was listening to the sound of voices and snatches of music. Some of the voices he knew.

It was a strange way to conduct a murder investigation.

Chapter One

Tony Young

I organized my first club when I was fifteen. It was for boys interested in birds; it lasted six months, but for the last four I was the sole member.

I did better with the next. The Harper Road Fan Club for Tommy Steele. We had twenty-five members, all contributing, monthly typed hand-outs and occasional meetings. But the meetings weren't so important, it was the thought between us that counted. Then there was the Radio Ham Club and the Philatelists' Club. I'm not a stamp collector but a club collector and I was getting liberal in my tastes. The next year I tried Young Lads for Labour. But this was kids' stuff. I hadn't got on to the big things yet.

Fate directs you, that I strongly believe. All these earlier efforts were training me for what was to be my real work. I won't say life work because my life hasn't run so far and there are lots of surprises in this package for everyone. Who can say what there really is in the universe? I'm a boy with a lot of faith, a good deal of it in myself. Some people say this is egotistical, but that's not how it is at all. If you have faith in yourself, stands to reason you have a lot of faith for other things too. I have plenty. I can feel myself reaching out. Maybe there is someone sitting on some medium hot star somewhere sending out messages to me. The light years problem worries me a bit. I mean that message started out when my ancestors were just crawling out of the slime so it can't really have my name on it. Or can it?

I like to think of that message winging its way through the centuries before I was born with my name on it. Tony Young, it would say. But there is what people call an 'area of sensitivity' about a thought like this and at the moment I am highly sensitive.

I always have been.

'You're a sensitive boy,' Mr Plowman said once, and he was absolutely dead right. I am a sensitive boy. I hated it when he died. If he is dead, that is. There's another sensitive area.

You might have thought that Mr Plowman and I would have cut across each other because he was an executive man like me. But no, once he realized how good I was in the organizational area he left it all to me and devoted himself to the spiritual side.

I soon had this new Club going like a bomb and I made the heart of it our meetings. I sensed right away that with this lot it was the meeting that counted. For the same reason I insisted all members were on the telephone; we had to be in contact. It was the contact of our minds that counted. All told I don't suppose we had more than a dozen members. There was a tight little inner bunch and then a number on the periphery. It wasn't the size of membership that made this my biggest operation so far, but our potential. For what we were after was the universe. Leave us alone and we might have our members strung out in the galaxies. And some of us thought we already had.

But don't misunderstand me. We were scientific in our approach. Nothing we regarded as *proved*. We just didn't have closed minds, that's all. Any report of an unidentified flying object being sighted and we took it seriously. We didn't laugh things off. Some were checked and got through our tests. Others, however much we might want to accept them, might fail on some little point of detail in our test and would have to be dismissed. I had it beautifully worked out. A report of a UFO appeared in the press and was given to one of our members; they telephoned it to me. I got in touch with Plowman, and Plowman and I appointed two agents to go out into the field and check. Sometimes he'd go himself, although he was better on the theory than on the practical. I hardly ever went, just sometimes, to see if the machine was running smoothly. I'm entirely an organization man. What John Plowman tried to do was to place his mind completely at the disposal of anyone or anything trying to get in touch with him; he wanted to be a focus.

He was too. He gave all his spare time to being a focus. Once a week on a Tuesday we all met in his house and his wife gave us cake and tea and we waited for John to give his report. Sometimes there wasn't much. Sometimes nothing at all, but sometimes he'd say he had a strong feeling that if we went to the coast just outside Dover, or stood on the road leading towards Bath (his feelings always came clothed in precise detail) then we should see something. I didn't usually go on these expeditions, but sometimes I'd take my girl friend along and we'd go together. I can't say I ever saw anything but on the other occasions, when I wasn't with them, the others frequently did. Once they saw four UFOs flying in formation and they dipped in salute over John's head.

I'd have given a good deal to have seen that, but no. Three of our most dedicated members were present that night: Esther Glasgow, a sweet girl but a little too inward-turning for my taste, Cyrus Calways Read (known as Cy) and old Miss Jones.

If anyone deserved a viewing Miss Jones did. She was going into hospital within the next few days for a serious operation and we all knew she might not come out. She was being very brave about it, though, and had promised to see what soundings the unconscious mind could pick up while under the anaesthetic. If the worst came to the worst and she became disembodied she was going to try to observe and pass on what information she could. She didn't promise anything. She was a very honest woman, old Miss Jones.

I thought Cy didn't seem too contented after this last viewing. I would never call Cy a really satisfied person; there was usually a worm or two eating at him.

'Touches of unfairness here and there,' he grumbled. We often walked home together. He lived just near my home. He had introduced me to John Plowman. 'Touch of favouritism, I'd say.'

'I don't see that.'

'I'm not as close to John as I ought to be. I don't feel the flow between us. Perhaps it's his wife. I feel she is rather *dark*.'

'She dyes it, I think. Touches it up, anyway.'

'I mean *spiritually*. You don't *believe* really, do you?' He gave a sharp look at me.

'I'm an organization man,' I said, not committing myself. 'Anyway, what did you mean by favouritism?'

'Oh, you'll find out. Goodbye. This is where I turn off.'

Our part of London isn't the best part of London to live but it has a certain cosiness. It's near the river and the docks, and the sea-gulls come racing in when there's bad weather out at sea. I wouldn't say I'm fond of it and a boy of my ambitions plans to get out of it, but I reckon even when I've left I'll come sometimes to say hello. Of course, it's changing fast and I dare say if I do come back I won't recognize it.

I live in Harper Road, Cy lives across the little square

– we call it the Banjo – in Peel Terrace. There's a subtle class distinction, which naturally I despise, between Peel Terrace and Harper Road. Harper Road is one step lower down in the social scale than Peel Terrace. You wouldn't know it walking past, but the people who live there, we know it. Mind you, you can rise in the world, you can put out window boxes and paint the front gate white and count yourself as good as Peel Terrace. My family haven't risen in the world. My father preferring birds to flowers in boxes and watching television to painting his gate white. You might even say we'd sunk because we did once have a sundial in the middle of our front garden, but my sister took it away and made it a tombstone for her old dog. He didn't die at the time, in fact he isn't dead yet, but his name is painted on it in blue paint and also the date when he didn't die. Against this, you could say that I, single-handed, have given us a kick upwards. I'm known as that clever red-haired boy that lives in Harper Road, or as "that mad one". Of course, I know what they call me. I heard plenty during the short period when I took a job as night-watchman in a local factory so as to have more time during the day. I work days now. I chose not to go to university. My sort of life doesn't need learning.

Around the corner from Peel Terrace and Harper Road a great new complex of building is going up. They've knocked down the old jam factory and in its place is a new jam factory, a quadrangle of shops that they call a shopping precinct and two new office blocks, including a police station which in my opinion is a luxury. The jam factory is finished but nothing else yet. The building has been going on for nearly two years, and one way and another it touches all our lives. We often smell of strawberries round here in the season.

'Good job they don't make kipper jam,' I said to Cy. He started. 'Kipper jam,' I repeated. 'Or we'd smell of that.' He didn't laugh. He has no sense of humour. A good-looking wife, four daughters, the only man to have seen four UFOs dip in salute and no sense of humour. It frightens you. 'You couldn't make kipper jam,' he said. 'There's no pectin in it.'

Although he'd said goodbye and hadn't laughed at my joke, he didn't seem to want to let me go. We stood at the corner, looking at each other.

'See you next week,' he said, without moving.

'Same time. I'll have it all written up by then. We might get this one in the press.'

'John doesn't want publicity.'

'He hasn't said so.' I was thinking how a bit of publicity would buck Miss Jones up. Publicly she would deplore it, inside it might be her last big thrill. Why shouldn't she have it, if I could give it to her?

'John's *always* against publicity,' Cy said firmly.

'Maybe.' No one knew what John thought, we only knew what he said he thought.

'What do you get out of this?' Cy said suddenly.

I was right, then, he did want to talk.

'Work. Interest. Information.' I shrugged.

'It's not enough.'

'I think it is.'

'I mean to explain you. You're young.'

'Oh, you're hard. If not on me, then on yourself. Relax. You want drums and parades and heads off all the time.'

'I'm serious about it all, I admit that. If that's a fault. I've got a scientific mind. You can't do work like mine without having a scientific mind.' I'd forgotten the work he did. Drove a van. I suppose it did need a scientific

14

mind. 'It worries me how unscientific some of the others are.'

'It's a subject with a lot of emotion in it,' I reminded him. 'You've got to reckon with that.'

He still looked angry.

'I reckon we take it all very calmly all things considered. That's John Plowman.'

'Oh, John.' He bit back his words. I was junior; he wasn't going to discuss John with me. He was naturally protocol-minded. It went with being scientific, I suppose. Scientists always think they've got a hot line straight through to God. 'You know I was the first person in the whole group to make serious checks. The first. The others came later. And I had the first photograph.'

Light dawned. 'You're jealous.'

He flushed. 'That's it, that's exactly what I'm complaining about. You just naturally think in terms of emotions.'

'All right. Emotion's out,' I said peaceably. 'No jealousy.'

As we stood there talking a policeman walked by, studying us unobtrusively as he passed. Hang about the streets these days and that's what you get. It's been this way ever since our troubles started in this district. Particularly for men, any age group.

'Good night,' said Cy, hastily. 'Next week then.' He walked off.

Cyrus's job was not heavily intellectual and there was no doubt he resented it, even though he did say it needed a scientific mind. He sold ice-cream from a Kandy Kream Kart which he also drove. And don't think the police hadn't investigated him pretty thoroughly just lately. He and his van were a natural for the sort of trouble we were in. But he was clear. The van was painted fondant pink and Cy wore a blue overall. I'd often wondered why he didn't hold down a better sort of job.

'Next week,' I called.

The policeman watched me go into my house. He knew me all right, but that wouldn't stop him watching me. They thought it was a local, you see. With these child crimes it's nearly always someone the kid knows. This is what gets them off their guard. There are other factors; I'll go into them some other time.

The Club was in a peculiar mood this last week, and that worried me. I'm obliged to be responsive to mood. I have to see the danger signals before anyone else. Today it seemed to me these signals were being run up from certain quarters. Of course, we'd never been what I'd call a *united* group, each of us approaching the common aim from a different viewpoint, from Miss Jones's open-minded optimism to John Plowman's detached belief. In the centre were three or four members, like Esther, who were convinced that all UFOs were genuine for emotional reasons. Cy was right there. These people believed because the idea of little men flying in from space fascinated them. They were living out a fairy-story they'd read when they were kids. Oh, I knew that all right. I say nothing about Cy's claims to scientific rationalism because I was never quite sure how far this existed.

Esther Glasgow had objected to the report John had drafted and I had written; her friend Peter had objected to the letter I had written to a similar club in the USA. "Too cagey," he'd called it. The secretary (technically I'm secretary of the Club, in practice I'm everything that requires pen and paper) has to be. I form the public image. We don't want it formed in a crackpot image, do we?

Or do we? Yes, there was no doubt where the danger

was coming from. The central emotional block. And behind it I strongly suspected was Cy Read. He was jealous of John Plowman. I could see his point. After all, it was in John Plowman's name I corresponded with our contacts across the Atlantic and it was John Plowman who organized the sky-watching routines and got first chance to prove or disprove an "incident".

A brief conversation with John Plowman was worrying me also. To a limited extent he made me his confidant.

'Of course, one has to ask oneself about these visitors from space: what their intentions are. I've always assumed their interest in us was a benign one.' He looked uneasy. 'Just lately, I've wondered if we were wise to *rely* on this.'

I know I didn't answer, but I suppose he saw the look on my face.

'There seems to have been a concentration of activity in this district. We seem to be a focus,' he went on, 'and I don't feel the result has been towards tranquillity.'

It certainly was not. There was a bad feeling everywhere lately, arising from the matter of the children, of course.

'Indeed, I've been getting strong intimations that something was going to happen.'

'How? Where do you read these intimations?' I asked bluntly.

'Naturally they don't put it in the newspapers,' he said irritably. 'I receive it in my mind. We are to get some sort of *proof*. There will be a sign.'

'Yes, that is quite worrying,' I said, carefully keeping all feeling out of my voice. 'Any details?'

'Just an impression comes into my mind that it will relate to someone who thinks he can fly.'

'I only know one person round here who thinks he can

fly,' I said, surprised. 'And I thought he'd given the idea up.'

Butty. Tom Butt. Butty (as we sometimes called him in unkind reference to his over-large buttocks) was at school with me. Spotty, dirty, fat, he had all the stigmata of the born victim, and seemed to know it too. He went out of his way to set us off. Like telling us that he dreamt he could fly. Without a doubt there was a sexual pleasure in our sport with him, just as there was in Butty's dreams that he could fly.

'I'm not happy about it all,' observed John Plowman. 'These ideas I get disturb me.'

They disturbed me. Without committing myself one way or another to the behaviour of the visitors from space (which might be good or not good, we had to see), I was beginning to be anxious about our little group. Wasn't there a strong sexual element in our preoccupation? We were a focus for something all right. I did wonder exactly *what* we were letting out into the world. Or stimulating.

I hung my coat up and went into the kitchen where my sister, Jean, was sitting drinking tea. She looked up.

'Back from meeting your loonies?'

I'm afraid she's picked up that rough way of talking from my father. It won't get her anywhere. I didn't answer but poured myself a cup of tea and started to drink it. They weren't loonies. A little unusual perhaps in their interests, but not loonies, or I wouldn't be associated with them.

'Seen anything lately?'

'You know I've never seen anything,' I said. 'I don't even look. That's not my job.'

She snorted. Very few women can make that noise, but she could. 'What do you get out of it?'

18

The second person who had asked me that tonight. 'I'm practising,' I said, and sipped my tea.

'It was me that made that tea you're enjoying so much,' she said.

That's another thing she's learned from my father; how to make a good cup of tea. They're remarkably alike. There are just the three of us, me, elder sister, and my father. My mother died a long while ago. I half remember her. Some days more than others. And I suppose that's how it is with my sister too. Some days she looks more like the photograph of my mother and the other days not. I'm always frightened she'll get to look like my father.

'You're pretty,' I said.

'Why the compliment?'

'Oh, I don't know. Perhaps I'm a bit low-spirited tonight.'

'Oh.' She considered. 'Where's Judith?' Judith was my former girl friend. Former, since last night.

'We've split up.'

'Why?' There again she was like my father. She had to know why. No tactful silences. Still, it was easy to answer.

'She said I don't raise her spirits.'

'Oh.' Once again she considered. 'You raise mine. I often get a good laugh out of you.'

'Thanks.'

'Oh well, you'll get another girl.'

'I won't get one with a car. Not round here.' It was luck kaving pulled in one girl friend with an automobile in this neighbourhood. Hers was a beautiful little white Triumph convertible, too. You froze in it in winter (she never let you put the hood up) but you felt a real he-man in summer. We only had one summer together, me, Judith and the car.

'She still on the stage?'

19

'Resting. Trying out for a part tomorrow.'

I got up to go upstairs to my room. 'Dad out?'

'No. Out the back watching his birds.'

At the door, I said: 'Can I have the front room this day week?' Jean nodded.

The Club occasionally met here. When it did Jean served coffee and cake and popped in and out observing us. I think she rather enjoyed it. I've noticed that this family's pleasure tends to be vicarious. Jean watches me, I watch the Club and Dad watches his birds. I must check this tendency.

I enjoyed the Club meetings myself. When we were really functioning well, comparing notes, checking photographs, suggesting future projects, all of them looking to me for directions, I had the feeling of the chain of power stretching directly from John Plowman to me and going no further. That was how I wanted it in that group and that was what I meant by practice. We might be stretching out to other galaxies, but as far as I was concerned it was strictly an exercise in politics.

On my way upstairs I looked out of the window on the stairs and saw a police car go past. Three children in eighteen months and all living within one square mile of each other. Three children just gone. Sixpence in the pocket, ta ta, Mum. And then never seen again. She was the first, Shirley Boyle, aged eight.

I went on into my room and sat down on my bed. Jean didn't come into this room much; I dusted it and looked after my bed. Jean knew I liked my secrets.

I drew the curtains on the night. The police car came back down the road. This time I could see a man in the back. He had a solid official look. We have a high-ranking policeman living round the corner from us. He's called Coffin. He has a wife who is observed sharply by the old cats of the neighbourhood because she is an actress and this naturally alerts their moral sense. Judith was going to introduce us before we broke up.

Down below I heard the telephone ring. When I'm established in my chosen way of life I shall have a telephone in every room. I hate people shouting up the stairs for me.

'Coming,' I called.

'David,' she said, when I got to the bottom of the stairs.

'Hello, Slave.' I called him this. David Edmondstone was someone I'd known at school and then lost sight of for a bit. The last year we'd seen each other regularly. If we'd had fags at the sort of school we went to, Dave would have been my fag. When we were "streamed" (that was their jargon for a sorting out process according to ability) I was A and he was C; that was the measure of our relationship. But when he came back I was glad to see him. He sort of fitted into my life. There had been a hole vacant and he came into it.

'Hello, Tony. Long time no see.'

'Only yesterday. And talk English.' I'd never cure him of using second-rate slang.

He laughed. 'Tony, I want to talk, I'm excited.'

He sounded it. 'Well, what's excited you?'

'I've got a new girl. You ought to see her.'

'Good.' Perhaps this one will last. They didn't usually. I mean no one wants fidelity but his turn-over was too rapid. I don't know what he did to them. I didn't take literally his remark about seeing her. I knew he wouldn't let me see her; he never did.

'Where did you meet her?' Jean was waving at me not to make a long call of it, but Dave might go on for hours. 'Where are you speaking from?'

'Call-box outside Lowther's.' Lowther's was a big all-night chemists which was a great place for night birds (which Dave and I intermittently were) in the New Cut Road. Fine old slum it have been at one time but now it was a newly built disaster area. 'Oh, I met her around,' he said vaguely. 'You know.'

'If you're going to talk all night, let me know,' whispered Jean.

I scowled at her, nodding my head like a mandarin. She didn't know what to make of that and it kept her quiet for a bit. Always keep your signals contradictory, that's a good rule with an opponent. It puzzles them and they don't know what to do. Quite scientific really. All animals have aggression or submission signals which other animals of their kind recognize. The dog snarls or cringes. We smile and nod or else frown and clench our muscles. Then the other animal knows what to do. But mix the signals and this throws them.

'You two,' she muttered. 'I don't like to watch. I mean, it's such a funny way to live.'

This time I smiled but shook my head slowly from side to side. Jean went and sat down, still keeping an eye on me. Dave was getting quite frantic on the end of the phone.

'You there? You still there? Well, are you listening then? Well, it was a lovely night, lovely night . . . ' He was working himself up.

'Calm it down, boy. So what did you do?'

'Talked,' he said dreamily. 'We're going on talking, too.'

'Lovely,' I said. 'Is that all?'

'No, then I came home and baby-sat for my sister. Those kids were a drag. Then I came out to phone you.'

'It was a big evening then?'

'Yes. What about you?'

'Oh, Club, home, Jean, you know.' I darted a look at Jean who was still watching. It crossed my mind she was expecting a call herself. 'Cy get home?'

'Yes, he certainly did.' Stronger feeling than even that aroused by his girl friend coloured his voice. 'And wasn't he sour! Came in, sat down in his chair and started writing his notes. Didn't say good evening or thank you for staying here or anything. He makes me sick. So I came out.'

David Edmondstone was Cy's brother-in-law and he lodged with his sister and Cy. Dave had gone away for a time to work in Birmingham but now he was back. In a way it was through knowing Dave that I found my way into the Club. Of course, it wasn't really a club till it got me. More of a loose association of people with a common interest. It was me and John Plowman that shaped it.

'How have you soured him up?' asked Dave.

How had we?

'I didn't know he kept notes,' I said.

'Well, he does. After every meeting. And sometimes he puts things on a tape. Not always. Just every so often. Not that I've seen. But I've heard him talking away to himself.'

'How do you know he has a tape recorder?'

'I've had a look round.' Dave laughed. 'Maggie doesn't know. And every so often he talks into it.'

'How often?'

'Well, I'm not watching him *all* the time. Not only that wouldn't be right, it wouldn't be easy.' In a way Dave ran away from home when he went to Birmingham. He said it was because his sister beat him. I didn't exactly believe him but I dare say she might have done. Or there's Cy. Since you ask me about him, I've always thought he was

23

a bit of a sadist. I saw a strap hanging on the wall of their kitchen. And they don't have a dog as far as I know. Dave was a bit slow in those days. But when he got back he'd grown up a lot.

'Since I've been here he's only done it a few times. But I tell you what: sometimes I think he plays back things he's done earlier. Yes, I think so.'

'I wonder what he puts on it?' I thought he was probably keeping his own record of sightings and investigations and no doubt adding a few sharp words about me and John Plowman. He was creating a Club of One.

'He keeps it locked up,' said Dave regretfully. 'He's got a little case where he keeps things. Regular old Bluebeard is Cy.' He laughed.

This isn't the image I would have found if *my* sister had been married to him, but Dave's imagination was as limited as his mother's had been. I just remembered his mother. Her idea of bringing up a boy was to whack him soundly every so often. At intervals she would go away from home and disappear for a few months. I think they really got on better when she was away than when she came back. I had an idea that Dave was going to take after her and turn into a disappearer. He was shaping that way.

I was shifting round vaguely in this conversation with Dave, trying to get at something – I didn't quite know what. Perhaps Cy was up to something. I didn't know. I just felt a pool of unease inside me.

'I must go now,' said Dave, almost as if it had been me that kept him talking. 'Tomorrow?'

'Tomorrow,' I agreed, although I hadn't really made up my mind about tomorrow. I like to feel free.

Jean watched me finish the conversation. 'Good,' she said. 'You worry me, you two. Such a funny way to live.'

Personally, I thought hers was a funny way to live, always dreaming over the teapot. She was only twenty-two and pretty. And my dad's way, wasn't that funny, worrying over his birds' breeding habits?

I heard Dad coming in from the back. This hastened me.

'Remember, even a sad and lonely life can be beautiful,' I said, giving her a smile as I passed.

I went back upstairs, drew back my curtains so I could see the sky. Clearly not the kind of night for a sighting. Anyway, John didn't expect anything over this neighbourhood at the moment. There was something unfavourable about our position. Perhaps it was just all the policemen. He thought in the direction of the New Forest was the most likely spot. There were signs, he said.

It was always through John that our messages and first intimations of a sighting came. Afterwards Cy told us the scientific explanation and I wrote it up, but John knew all about it first. I wondered about this sometimes.

I took out my papers. I knew Jean worried about me. But she didn't need to. I had my life well arranged.

Like Cy I made notes and kept records. I had an account of all the weekly meetings. I had a brief on each sighting of a UFO involving a Club member. When a special expedition had been launched by John Plowman then I had it all down: how information of the incident reached us first, with times and dates, when the checking expedition set off, again with times and dates, and the results.

I looked at my notes, then raised my head to stare at the dark starless sky. I felt so alone, but I wasn't really alone, there were a hundred little dark figures tagging around with me. I have a very crowded memory. I feel sometimes that I can remember everything that happened to everyone in the whole wide world. But this can't be, it must just be that I'm a sensitive boy. Now I kept thinking about murder and there had to be a reason for it.

I knew why Jean was sitting hunched over her teapot.

The last child that had disappeared was a kid she taught. Did I tell you Jean was a teacher? Yes, she's a clever girl really. Brave, too, eight to eleven is the age range she specializes in. It's the best age, she says. When I asked for what, she simply smiled at me and let it go.

Had eleven been the best age for Katherine Gable? Katherine Gable, eleven last June, third of a family of nine. The only girl. On Thursday June 26 Katherine had eaten her supper and gone out to play with little friend Milly Lee in Saxe-Coburg Street. Little friend Milly had come home in due time and gone to bed. When questioned she said that she had only played a little while in Saxe-Coburg Street with Katherine. No one had seen Katherine again.

I remembered Thursday June 26. It was one of our big days. There had been a reported sighting near the Thames in Buckinghamshire and John and a select little party had driven out to see it. I wasn't quite sure who had been on that expedition. I should have to consult my records. Not me, not Miss Jones.

Katherine Gable on June 26.

May had been a clear month both for us and missing girls, but one day in late April – the 23rd – we'd had a sighting and another girl had gone missing. I knew the date because that was one UFO that had got into the papers and the two sensations got headlines side by side.

Grace Parker was only ten, but in her photograph she looked older. I never find it easy to guess a kid's age;

especially a girl kid. I would have said this one was around thirteen, but no, the newspapers said she was ten. She had elderly parents. Perhaps they let Grace run around more than she should. No one had found Grace, but they had found her scarf. It had been left hanging from a tree in the park. 'There's no need to wear a scarf tonight, Grace. It's a warm night.' And the answer, 'I like to wear a scarf, I feel comfortable with a scarf round my neck.' A blue and yellow scarf, a present from someone for Christmas, I knew that. It must have been in the newspapers. I'd never spoken to Grace, had I? Unlike the Katherine Gable affair, no one I knew had known Grace. But she was walking there in my mind, a tiny figure, seen as if through the wrong end of the telescope, with every feature perfectly clear.

I consulted my records. Spaced out among the six months behind me had been several Club expeditions. Nothing important, you understand. I suspected that one or two of the trips were arranged by John Plowman for his own amusement. At all events there had been UFO sightings. I already knew that two of these sightings coincided with dates on which two girls had disappeared. Katherine Gable on June 26 and Grace Parker on April 23. I had been turning this thought over and over in my mind and wondering what people would make of it if they knew. What *should* they make of it? What was true and what false?

Was it something you could brush off as just coincidence? Or were people going to think the girls had been kidnapped into space? Could you expect anyone to think that? *Should* they think it? I couldn't make up my mind.

Jean came into my room and dropped the old cat on to my bed, where he always slept.

'Sorry if I was irritable about Dave.'

'You weren't.'

She saw I looked troubled.

'I know I shouldn't interfere in these boy-to-boy relationships.'

'We don't have a boy-to-boy relationship.' I think one of the things that draws me to Dave is that we both started up acne at the same time. Mine has cleared; his hasn't.

'No.' She knew something was worrying me, but she didn't have any idea what it was. How could she? But she can catch on fast, can Jean, and she was watching me. Give her time and she'd read me like a book.

People think that boys like Dave and me don't understand. But it's not true; I know that if you've got someone like us, you've got a monkey in the family.

So I always tried to be good to Jean. Now I got up and offered her a chair, but she wouldn't stay. She never would. There was something about my room she didn't like. Me, probably.

'Don't talk too much tonight, Jean,' I said. 'Somehow I don't think it's a good night for talking.'

She left me alone. I went to the window and looked out. It was an ugly time for talking. An ugly night and I felt ugly with it.

There are so many crimes that no one gets to know about. 'The dark number', the police call it, don't they?

At the window I could just see the house where Dave lived with his sister and her husband in Peel Terrace. Although Peel Terrace rates itself above Harper Road they're so close together you could throw a stone from us to them. I wondered if Cy was sitting there dictating into his tape recorder. I looked at my own machine. The thought of all that tape whirring round gave me a funny feeling. They're dangerous machines, closer than a friend, easier to talk to than a woman, but terribly, terribly likely, at the flick of a switch, to tell all.

I started to play a tape. Strange noises began to play themselves out in my quiet room. I kept it low. I didn't want Jean to hear.

There were strange sounds on this tape.

Sometimes I think it sounds like a tiny, tiny girl, sometimes like a man. But crying, man and girl, both are crying.

One day I'll tell you how I got these sounds on my tape.

I'd like to tell someone. It's on my mind a lot.

Chapter Two

John Coffin

I know all about the dark number that Tony Young was talking about. As a serving police officer I have to. It's the Dark Number of Crime, the number of crimes that take place and never come to the attention of the police. Some criminologists think that the crimes that come into the open and get punished represent no more than 15 per cent of the crimes that are committed. That makes the dark number a good 85 per cent, which makes it a bad figure to go to bed on.

Every day I have to face the reality of the dark number. A criminal convicted of a small robbery asks for several other offences to be taken into consideration. Most of them are known to the police, but some of them are new. A scrap-iron dealer whose premises are being searched on suspicion of another crime turns out to have a neat little forging business running in a back room.

Tony Young and I both know that there's plenty of things going on in society that stay in the dark. There's an act of cruelty, probably against a child, going on now, at this minute while you listen to this.

I've encouraged Tony Young to speak freely, to put everything down that he wants to say and from listening so often to the important tapes I've come to feel the relief of talking into one myself. Also, it's practical. I can arrange my thoughts, form a picture better this way than any other. Yes, Tony Young's right when he says a tape is one's most receptive audience. Perhaps there's a danger to it. I can see you might get to trust it too much and it might start to stimulate the wrong centres of the mind. I think that happened with the maker of one of the tapes. Perhaps that one started out ordinary enough and ended up a monster. A monster bred from the tapes.

I learnt a lot of what makes a man a monster in the time that I was dead. The doctors say it was an illness following upon concussion but to me it was the time I died. Between the man who lived before and the man who lives now is a gulf, bridged only by the name John Coffin and the same body. And even this isn't quite the same body. Or else I fit in it differently.

However, I was glad enough to come back to life, death not being what I'd expected it to be. Back in life again, I discovered to my surprise that during my demise I had received promotion and become responsible for the detective bureau in a large area in a big police division in South London. So I was Superintendent Coffin with a few satellite inspectors. That was something to come back to life for.

My wife says I talk differently since I returned to the world. She says she can't put her finger on it but she's working on it and one day she'll tell me. So I have that to look forward to. It's this sort of thing that makes coming back to life worthwhile.

For the first three months of my renaissance I had a clear run. Crime and violence, oh yes, even a nicely planned bank robbery. (But it turned out the bank was undergoing a security inspection of some sort and didn't have much cash on hand. Still, we pulled in one or two old friends and put them away.) No crime in those few months, however, to make you feel sick.

I remember rejoicing. Even from the grave you bring back hope. A policeman too!

It was waiting in the wings though. And this is where

we get back to what I said about the dark number of crime. When the first small girl was reported missing, was this truly the first or was it just the first we heard about? If you've had no experience of the sort of society I'm talking about you'll say I'm crazy. 'What, a child go missing,' you say, 'and no one report it? Why, the parents'd be round there creating as soon as they could.' Well, in the first place, not every child has parents. And then secondly, the parents of any child do not always behave in the way you might expect. Especially the parents of a girl child. Especially mothers. I've met the whole range of mothers in my job, from good mothers and baddish mothers to downright wicked mothers, and there are a few poor damned souls who just get lost. So the picture that is in my mind is this: the first few girls who were missing came back. But they came back having been assaulted. Perhaps they didn't know quite what had happened to them. They don't want to talk about it. And the parents of these particular little girls being silly and fearful and ashamed just wrap it up. Tell no one and hope the child will forget. You could only offer them pity and despair.

So I am calculating that ahead of all the missing children we know about there is a dark number that we don't know about. The first case was probably relatively trivial. The next a bit worse. And so it built up.

Katherine Gable on June 26, Grace Parker on April 23, and a whole year previously, Shirley Boyle aged eight on March 18. What had happened in the year between? Was it the dark number operating? Were there in fact episodes in these months about which, for some reason or other, we knew nothing?

On the day after Christmas a girl called Kim Simpson had disappeared. She had come back, unharmed, but with nothing much to say about where she had been. Perhaps she was another.

And then there was the other. The disappearance that no one knew about yet.

'Anything wrong?' my wife said.

'No, nothing special,' I said. 'Just wondering where people go when you're not looking at them. And that's not a problem in philosophy. Just something Dove and I think about a lot lately.'

'Yes, of course. The children.' Little as she liked police work, she looked sympathetic and understanding, because after all, she *is* a mother. Not always a particularly good mother, but still a mother.

My wife didn't say any more. She's trying very hard to be tactful at the moment. She's temporarily out of work. Resting, as those in her trade call it, and this gives her a lot of time to be tactful.

All the children had come from the one small heavily populated area. Unluckily it's a district where the children play in the street and sit on the doorsteps. There's even a playground in a corner by the river. If anyone was hunting children he could have all he wanted in this district.

Even now, when mothers were on the alert, he wouldn't have to look around too much.

All the same, there was an eerie quality in the way the last incident had happened. One minute the child was playing in the street, the next the street was empty. Someone had come down in a fiery chariot and picked her up.

It was late afternoon. Not a bad day with my work going well. I was getting ahead with my paperwork, for which I have lately developed a taste. I used to hate it, but now it satisfied me to have everything orderly about me. A good enough day for me. I was glad to be alive. But a bad day, or no day at all for the parents of Katherine Gable and Grace Parker and the other girls. And only good for me because, for the moment, I had buried the thought of it, and could get down to the work which I had neglected because of it.

I had set up the mechanism, you see. I was at the controls of the machine investigating the disappearances, and I had Inspector Dove to back me up and we both had the assistance of that stout young sergeant with the red hair called Parr who got the Police Medal last year. You saw him in the paper, I expect. He wasn't a great brain but he was thorough. And I am thorough and Dove is thorough and we were getting help from any scientific and technical bureau we wanted to tap but still we were getting nowhere.

The girls had gone, one on a sunny afternoon, another on a cold spring day, the third in the evening. We knew the people who would admit to seeing them last and that was all we did know.

And, of course, this wasn't all I had to worry about. There was a suspected case of arson in a local mosque; an illicit drug trader trying to set up a centre in a hostel down by the docks; and someone was unloading fake half-crowns in all the pubs in the district.

One of my office windows overlooked Saxe-Coburg Street, which is a busy road off New Cut Road. I could see New Cut Road from my other window. It wasn't a view any tourist would rave about and no one had painted it, but I was fond of it. A good deal of my life had been built around Saxe-Coburg Street. I'd been walking up and down it all my life. I'd seen it in war when the bombs dropped on it and I saw it now in prosperity. Because it was prosperous, make no mistake about that. It was getting the taste of big wages and steady employment and enjoying it. On all sides there were prophets of every sort of doom, economic and moral, but Saxe-Coburg Street couldn't help appreciating the virtues of a world which gave it refrigerators, motor cars and cheap birth control. When the road had been run up by a speculative builder to celebrate the Prince Consort's Great Exhibition of British wealth not even the Queen in her palace had had the benefit of any of these and Saxe-Coburg Street knew it.

My room was dark and small. I was probably the last policeman who was going to work in it. Across the road they were building a new police station for us. Every day I watched its progress with interest. Sometimes (like the day they had a fire) it seemed to go backwards and not forward, but equally sometimes it shot forward and I could even imagine us moving into it. Not today, though. The site looked deserted and I could only see one man working there. He seemed to be working in a workman's lift running up the front of the building; it had reached the fifth floor. Did I tell you we were to have a tall, narrow, police building? I believe I was scheduled to have an office on the third floor. I hoped I'd still have my view.

I could see Saxe-Coburg Street with a professional eye too, of course. It's not exactly the road where you'd leave your car unlocked, or leave the cream too long on the step; someone would nick it. But you probably could send the baby toddling out with a five-pound note to buy your paper and she and the change would come back unscathed. There was a great love of children in Saxe-Coburg Street and neighbourhood, due perhaps to a wave of Italian immigrants it had had at the turn of the century, whose descendants, cockneys to a man, were still there.

Until now I would have said the child was as safe in our district as it could be anywhere. That wasn't so very safe perhaps, but until now it hadn't been downright lethal.

Inspector Dove gave my door his usual swift knock which didn't wait for an answer and sat down, again without waiting to be asked. He looked tired. He was hoping for promotion and was working hard on this account, as well as being genuinely anxious about the missing children.

'Like that?' I said.

'It's always like that.' He was usually gloomy, anyway in speech, and at work. I dare say he sparkled at home. But he was a good policeman. We had known each other a good many years and a lot of the memories that were written on my face were written on his too. Perhaps he thought I was gloomy too and that I sparkled at home.

'I hate these kid cases.'

'Don't we all?'

He got to his feet and went and looked from the window.

'I'd like to believe it's an outsider coming in, but I don't believe it.' He rapped on the window. 'It's someone in that area out there, someone local, that's responsible.'

'What makes you so sure?'

He turned round from the window and came back to stand in front of me.

'Not one thing. Lots of little things.'

'Such as?'

He took a deep breath. 'The way the kids go. First you see them, then you don't. If that had happened once I'd take it as luck, but it's happened every time. No one has seen the child go. No one has seen a stranger come up and speak to her, no one has seen any unusual contact, no one has seen anything.'

'So?'

'That must mean it's a local. Either someone so well known he fades into the background, or someone who knows every inch of the ground round here, and how to take advantage of it. I think he must have known the children too.'

'Where are the children then?' I asked.

'Yes, you'd think we'd have found a trace of them, wouldn't you?'

'If they haven't been taken out of the district, yes, I would.'

'But we haven't. They're dead. Packed up somewhere in something. Even buried. But dead.'

'So we check the neighbourhood.'

'But that takes time, John, and I can't wait.'

We were both silent, because this was the terrible worry; that while we were working another child would go.

'Perhaps something will turn up to give us a lead.'

'Not from this lot, John; with them there's been nothing. So if you're looking for anything it must be with another child.'

'Who have you had a look at?' I said.

'Every crawler in the neighbourhood.' Crawlers were what we called the sex offenders. We had our share. Lately more seemed to be moving in. Perhaps we were building up a coven. 'And they all are covered. Either in hospital, in prison or well chaperoned.'

'Someone could be covering for them.'

'Yes, there's always that,' he agreed. 'Or else it's a new one we don't know.'

'There's usually a beginning to that sort of thing,' I said. 'Something that stands out in the way of oddness, even if it's only wearing a hat where you don't usually wear a hat.'

'I've even checked them. Even the man who sells papers at the corner and swears at everyone who comes past. The kids tease him.'

'Might be something there.'

'Could be. I'm not crossing him off. He's a woman, by the way.'

'Oh.' It was surprising what you turned up when you started looking. 'Well, I didn't know that.'

'No, even his mother didn't. Used to put him in trousers. Her, I mean. But I'm still no nearer,' he went on.

It meant we were missing something, of course. We had our fair proportion of nuts in the neighbourhood, you can't help it in a district like ours. We also had our share of crank organizations. In fact, we were rather above average there. We had a sociologist from London University down here once doing a survey to find out why, but all the conclusion he could come to was that we just had them the way other districts had rats. So I knew all about Tony Young's Club of UFO watchers. I had them on my list and thought them pretty harmless, although undoubtedly they were going to be useful if a flying saucer landed in my bailiwick. But when such organizations get mixed up with young men like Tony Young they are asking for trouble. From Tony Young's description perhaps you haven't got quite the right picture of the Club. Let me consolidate it for you. To begin with, he didn't quite invent its organization the way he thinks he did. Secondly, he isn't quite the powerful figure in it he believes. He's using them all right, but they are using him too. Ask me how I know. I've met John Plowman before. Before he became interested in UFOs, he had been investigating the possibility of radio signals from beings in outer space. He showed a long and protracted interest in that subject, but I don't know that he ever got anywhere. He had a little group of about six or seven working with him, some of whom went on to form the nucleus of the UFO group. And before that he housed for six months a woman who said she was the channel through which beings from Venus could pass into this earth world. He investigated her claim while she stayed as his guest, but I don't know what he discovered and she dematerialized one day. Or so he supposed, but he never quite committed himself to belief. I'm almost sure I saw her eighteen months later in Lewisham Road, but perhaps not. So although John Plowman had some strange interests he was perfectly consistent in them and carried out his investigations in a thorough, detached way. I believe he had a degree in engineering from London University.

You may wonder why, if he's so harmless, I continue to take an interest in him. Pehaps because it's my job, you can never tell when one thing is going to branch out into another and I believe in preventing crime; and perhaps because he picked up some strange characters on his way.

So I knew about John Plowman and his group and as soon as we ran into trouble I had the idea of looking at them afresh. I though of calling in that young sociologist again. When all is said and done, a policeman is only as good as his informers, and in a specialized world like John Plowman inhabits I have to have a special sort of informer. I don't suppose my sociologist would like to be called an informer. But if I use him (and I probably will use him) that's just what he'll be, one of a fellowship made up of men like Frank Bowen (aged forty; at least half of those years spent in prison. Incompetent but hopeful. Perfect for my purposes); little Ned Thaw (a liar, but so stupid that even his lies showed me the truth, like the other side of the coin), and smiling, bad-tempered Happy Boy Hooper whom nobody liked.

'I'll do some asking around,' I said to Dove.

'Thanks.' He knew what I meant. He stood up to go. 'They're getting on with that building over the way,' he said. 'I suppose we'll be in it soon. I shan't be sorry. This place is falling down round our ears. Know what I heard. The rats from here have moved into the new building in time to meet us.' He was quite serious. He was one of those people who find rats deeply interesting. So did I, for that matter.

'Wonder what they're living on?' I gathered my papers together, preparatory to leaving. I should have to come back in later this evening, but I could have an hour at home. I was hungry too. This was what made me wonder what the rats were eating.

'Wood shavings, debris, food the workmen leave behind. Or they bring stuff in. They're clever boys, those rats are. There's a delicatessen next door.' He was full of admiration for the rats' skill.

'Remind me not to shop at that delicatessen.' I was ready to go. 'Wait for me, I'm coming along.'

We went out of the building and into the street together. You never know what you're walking into.

There was a group standing on the pavement by the half-completed building: a small group made up of six men and one woman. They were staring upwards.

'What's this?' said Dove.

Before we could walk across a boy detached himself from the group and ran across to us.

'There's a man up there in trouble,' he said, pointing upwards to where, high on the structure of scaffolding, the lift-cage was. 'He's stuck,' he said breathlessly. He was a boy of about seventeen wearing working clothes.

We joined the group and looked up. It was still daylight but it had been one of those sultry, overcast days you get so often in London. You really couldn't see much. I could see the cage and make out a shape.

'Why's he crouching there?' said the woman.

'Is he crouching?' I wasn't sure what I could see.

'He was standing up a little while ago, I swear it. Now he's on his knees. He's ill.' She was breathless with interest. 'That's what it is, he's been taken ill.'

'How did it happen?'

'Well, I don't know. I was just coming by with my shopping when this young boy says there's a man stuck up there.' She looked round for the boy, who nodded vigorously.

'Yes, he's up there,' he said, with interest and apparent pleasure.

'Supposing he falls down?' said the woman.

'No, he won't fall down. It's like a great cage, see.'

'How did it happen?' I asked, stepping back to get a better look, but it wasn't easy to get details clear at that angle.

The boy shrugged. 'He phoned down to me and said: Help me, help me, they're getting me.'

'That was a funny thing to say.'

'I didn't know what he meant. And I said: Come down, then. And he said: I can't, the power's gone. Then he said he was falling.'

'But he hasn't fallen.' I squinted upwards, trying to see.

'It doesn't make sense,' agreed the woman.

'I think the lift's stuck,' said the boy.

'It was working all right this morning,' said one of the

other men, turning round to talk. 'Much you know about it, Patsy Burden.'

'I know what I'm told,' retorted Patsy.

'And what's been done about it?' I aked. I was beginning to think the man up there *was* ill. Or worse.

'I heard him call out,' said the woman, reading my thoughts, 'when I got here first. He's dead silent now.'

'I got the foreman coming,' said the boy.

'I reckon he's dead.'

'The foreman's coming,' repeated the boy.

'He's not God, is he?' demanded the woman. 'Supposing the poor chap's gone, he can't bring him back.'

'He's not gone,' said the boy. 'I see him.' He pointed.

'Not gone in that way, stupid. Gone, passed away. Dead.'

I was still silent. I had that itchy, scratchy feeling I get when things are going wrong. I scratched my wrist absently. I'd had an infection there once and my skin still remembered it.

'Here *is* the foreman,' said Dove. 'It's Joe Davies. I know him. Hello, Joe, trouble here?'

'There shouldn't be,' said the foreman, a tall spare man with a brush of fair hair. 'But this lot can foul up anything.' He glared at the bunch of men. 'Have you tried bringing it down?'

'No,' said one of the men. 'I saw one of those cages drop from top to bottom once with the man in it. *You* do it.'

'Who is it up there? Whoever it is he shouldn't be there. We're not working that face today.'

'I bet he's thinking he shouldn't be there.'

'I think it's Tom Butt,' said one of the men.

'And what's Butty doing up there?'

'I dunno. Anyway, he's a nervous type. If he went up there it was because someone told him to.'

'I'll give him nervous when I get him down.' He moved away.

'I'll come with you, Joe,' said Dove.

'Thanks.' But he hardly looked at Dove as he strode off. We both followed him towards a small wooden hut which stood at the bottom of the scaffolding.

It was empty, but smelt of men in sweaty clothes and cigarette smoke and stale tea.

'I have all the controls here,' said Joe. He looked white. He put out a hand towards a panel of switches, then hesitated. 'Maybe I should get the police.'

'I *am* the police, Joe,' Dove reminded him.

'How does the lift work?' I asked.

'By electricity. We don't pull it down by hand.' He was irritable. 'He has a control up there. I have an emergency switch down here.'

'How can you get in touch?'

'We have a telephone.' He pointed at it. 'But either it's gone dead or he's not answering. I've tried to get him three times.'

'Pull that emergency switch.'

'If that man gets killed . . . '

'Yes,' said Dove gently.

'Why is this hut empty?' I said. 'Shouldn't there be someone here?' It looked like the technological heart of the building operation.

'Yes, me,' said Joe briefly. 'And the boy's about. He took the call.'

'Pull the switch, Joe,' advised Dove. 'And quickly. If the power is on then that cage will come down safely. If it's not then it'll stay put; it won't fall.'

Joe still hesitated.

'Get him down,' said Dove.

I was letting Dove take charge because he knew the man.

Without another word, Joe reached out and pulled down a red-coloured lever.

'Go outside and watch,' he said, now calm. 'I'll stay here.'

When we rejoined the watching crowd it had grown in size. There was a pause and then the cage began to descend, slowly at first and then more swiftly. The crowd sighed with relief.

Gathering speed the cage slid towards the ground. I thought it was travelling just fractionally too fast for safety.

I looked at it and looked again.

The cage slid to the pavement. But this time we had all seen. There was a heap of crumpled clothes in a corner and a pair of shoes, but otherwise the cage was empty.

The woman gave a little tiny muted shriek.

We could see a jacket, some shoes, a shirt, and a white protective helmet. But Tom Butt was gone. He had left his clothes and disappeared.

Chapter Three

John Coffin

On the corner of Saxe-Coburg Street and Harper Road we examined the clothes. I didn't know what to make of the episode. It was a strange thing, but the clothes were there all right.

An old pair of working trousers, not too dirty all things considered, a short-sleeved shirt and a woollen cloth jacket with a zip up the front. There was also a pair of black leather shoes with rubber soles. The shoes were pretty worn.

'Tom's clothes,' said one of the men. 'That's his jacket, anyway. About the shoes and shirt I couldn't say.'

I ran my hand through the pockets of the jacket and drew out a few coins and a letter folded in two.

The letter was addressed to Tom Butt and the address was a hostel in Farmer Street. I knew the place. I looked at the envelope, but decided not to open it just yet. It was still Tom Butt's private life. He still had one. We'd let him keep it as long as we could.

No one knew better than me that his chances of keeping it, under certain circumstances, were slim.

'Yes, they're Tom Butt's,' I said. I folded the clothes and handed them back to Joe the foreman. 'You better keep these for the time being.'

'But you're the policeman.'

'I don't know that there's a case for us here.'

'But where's Tom?'

I shrugged. 'Wherever he is he's got on his under-clothes and a pair of socks.'

'And his overalls,' put in one of the onlookers. 'He wore overalls over that lot.'

'And some overalls, then,' I said.

'But where's he gone?'

'Your guess is as good as mine. Perhaps better. Where's he likely to have gone?'

'But how could he go? One minute he's calling out for help from the top of the building and the next he's gone. How could he go?'

'Well, he didn't walk,' I said. 'And I don't suppose he could fly.'

'If he didn't come down, then I bet he's up there still. He could hardly crawl through the bars of the cage. He must have lost his nerve,' said Joe, turning back to look at the shell of the building. 'Search the place, boys, and shout as you go, so as I'll hear.'

Dove was very quiet and so was I, but we eyed each other. Dematerialization wasn't something we'd worked with much.

'If there's a screwy situation, there's a screwy answer,' muttered Dove. 'But there's an answer.'

He was right, but it wasn't always an answer you wanted to hear.

They searched the building site from top to bottom but there was no sign of Tom. But rolled up in a bundle, not far from the cage, they found some overalls. They were reasonably clean and not stained or torn in any way; they appeared to be Tom's. So now, wherever Tom was, he didn't have overalls either. It was a perplexing thought.

'Like I said, there's an answer,' said Dove. 'Just wait and he'll come walking in.'

'You may be right.'

'Or he won't come walking in. He'll be carried in. Or

we won't ever see him again, but there'll be a picture and we shall know how or why.'

It was because he really believed this that Dove was a good policeman. He never took no for an answer. But sometimes he had to put up with two answers and not knowing which one was right.

Joe came back, looking worried.

'My God, I don't know what's become of him,' he said. 'It's like he's been snatched up to heaven. Where's that boy Patsy Burden? What was it he said to you? Tell us again, Patsy.'

'He called, "Help me, help me, they're getting me". That was the first time. And I said, "Come on down then". And he said, "I can't, the power's gone".'

'Only it hadn't,' said Joe.

'No. And then he said, "Help me, help me, I'm falling".'

'I don't know. It's mad.'

He looked up at the building. 'He's our first casualty. If he is one. On a big site like this the building always gets one or two. But this is the first time anyone's absolutely got eaten up.'

'That's a strange way of putting it,' I said.

'Well, it's what it looks like, isn't it? If one thing's certain it's just that he didn't fall.' He stared upward again, then shrugged.

'He'll be back,' said Dove, maintaining his unshakeable belief in the laws of the universe. But perhaps the laws of this world don't hold good for all other worlds. There might be a way on what the scientists call the "space-time continuum" for a solid block of earth-matter called Tom Butt to disappear from our view.

He might be gone and yet still be there. Perhaps he could hear us.

'Call his name,' I said suddenly. 'Call his name. Tom! Tom Butt!'

We all called, once, twice and three times, but the wind brought his name dustily back to us and there was no other sound.

'A weird little business,' I said. 'But nothing to do with us.'

'No. Nothing. Leave him alone, and he'll come walking in.'

Certain things are clearer to me, now that I am getting this on the tape, than they were at the time, and one is that Dove was putting on an act. He was not altogether genuine in his portrayal of an unimaginative down-to-earth policeman. Underneath he was already deeply disturbed.

'I'll give you a lift home,' he said. He was proud of his car, which was new. 'It's over here.'

'Thanks, but I think I'll walk.' It was only just round the corner. And I think better walking. There seemed plenty to think about.

'Wait a minute,' he said furiously. 'My car's gone. It's been lifted.'

There were cars in plenty lining the kerb, but his car, smart and shining, was gone. Those that were left had suffered a little from their life in London.

He was white with rage. 'Come on, let's report it missing and start things moving.' He stamped forward. 'God, I'm angry,' he said.

But after his first outburst, he didn't say much. My wife complained I was silent that evening. Probably Dove's wife did the same. I suppose he spoke about his car, but I don't believe he said much else.

'No, different,' I remember I answered my wife when she had asked me if this case was like the case of the missing children. This wasn't quite true. I was wondering if there was not some similarity.

We had set up a temporary headquarters for the missing children investigations in a small house annexed to the station. We had to have a special place because we were getting a lot of outside help. By which I mean that everyone who knew something that might help or thought they did or hoped they did called us and wanted to talk. I don't blame them, in a case like this it's almost inevitable, but it makes work harder. You have to listen to them, but all the time you know that the person who could tell you something is keeping quiet (because almost certainly there is a wife or a mother or a sister who could tell you a lot) and yet you listen, because the very flow of these stories puts pressure on the silent one, which in the end is going to break her. I say her, but it could be him. Usually it's a woman, though.

Dove had just finished a briefing session with the detectives assigned to the case when I came in next day.

'Nothing,' he said straight away. 'There isn't anything new.'

'But you thought there might be?'

'Well, I was hoping.'

'Anything new on Tom Butt?'

'He hasn't turned up, if that's what you mean,' Dove said in a sour tone.

'Well, we don't have to look for him, do we?' I sat down at Dove's desk. All his papers were thrown about. I could see he'd doodled a huge circle on a piece of paper and then dug a hole in it with a pencil. It was how he felt, I suppose. Inside a circle and he'd got to dig himself out. It was how I felt too, come to think of it.

'No one's yet *asked* us to look for Tom Butt. He's an adult and can go where he likes.'

'Eighteen,' I said. 'Just eighteen and a nervous type. Not such an adult. And in a strange country.'

'I'm wondering now if he isn't in a stranger one,' said Dove.

'Hasn't it struck you that there's a resemblance showing up between the way Tom Butt went and the way the children went?'

'And lots of points of difference too.'

'And that that's the stranger country he's now in.'

'It did occur to me,' admitted Dove, 'but it's ridiculous.' He walked around the room. This house had once been a small school and it still had blackboards round the walls which we used. Dove had written a list of dates on them.

> Thursday June 26, 1969.
> Wednesday April 23, 1969.
> Monday March 18, 1968.

I knew what these dates stood for: they were the dates of the last three disappearances.

'It's ridiculous,' Dove repeated, turning his back on the dates. 'He just left, that's all. He wasn't taken. He just left.'

I went over to the blackboard and wrote the day before's date on it. 'There, if Tom Butt comes back, we can rub it off. Otherwise, it stays.'

'Either he'll turn up or he won't turn up,' said Dove, with a shrug. 'Either we'll find out all about it or we won't find out about it. That's how I feel.'

But Coffin felt a little sick.

Chapter Four

At this stage Coffin had only the one tape, his own. He played it over to himself because it seemed to him he had thoughts and words down on it that were useful. Dove was shrugging his shoulders but Coffin was uneasy.

He was surprised to realize how much he (and Dove too for that matter) seemed to be reaching forward to put into speech things they didn't quite understand. Why for instance had they both seized on that phrase 'A strange country'? Perhaps it was he and Dove and not Butt who were in a strange country.

Tom Butt, aged eighteen, five feet four inches tall, weighing 140 pounds, had disappeared into thin air. He had gone from a closed cage stuck up high on the building, flying away like a bird.

He was a man in a puzzle. If you could think of him like that then you reduced the human element.

But nothing could reduce the human element in the case of the missing children and it would be obscene to try.

Coffin put the tape in a drawer and got back to the routine of his day. He had reports to read, three reports to dictate and in forty minutes he had to attend a conference to be held in another division about the amnesty of firearms. He was going to be late for this conference.

And in his opinion there were still plenty of firearms floating around his bailiwick that the amnesty wasn't going to touch. No amnesty was going to make a man give in a gun that he had paid for, polished, worn next to his skin and, whether he knew it or not, was looking forward to using. Only the people who were never going to use a gun were going to be influenced by any police offers of oblivion. At the most, you removed a few outmoded weapons and left behind the really lethal equipment. He could think of at least two men who almost certainly had a nice little armoury left.

'Charley Barnes for one,' he said aloud thoughtfully. 'He was looking pretty cheerful the other day down the Blue Anchor.' The Blue Anchor was the local street market. Charley had certainly been looking cheerful and his wife had been wearing a mink wrap. Of course, mink was getting cheaper, but still . . . 'It might be an idea to make him less cheerful. Might get a search warrant and have a look round.'

He made a note to start this ball rolling and at once felt more cheerful himself.

Out of his window he could see a uniformed constable walking along the row of parked cars and testing the doors to see if they were locked: he interpreted this as the arm of Inspector Dove reaching out. He hadn't seen his colleague today, but the grapevine reported that his car had not yet been returned.

Also out of his window he saw an untidy straggle of children headed by a teacher pass on their way from the new swimming pool on the main road to their old school (due, like the police station, for imminent demolition). He had long eyesight and recognized the teacher in charge as Jean Young. He had interviewed her over the disappearance of Katherine Gable. Anyway, they were old acquaintances and enemies. At the age of ten she had asserted her defiance of law and order by heaving a stone through one of his windows. In a way she was heaving them still.

Coffin looked at her with something like sympathy. She headed every action group in the district, marched on every protest march and had organized the petition against police cruelty when the Peace Marchers had camped down by Daffodil Fields (no daffodils but a good square of concrete), but she had had to be mother and practically father as well to her brother Tony since her mother had died. He looked at her organizing her flock to cross the road. No doubt about it, there was a lot of maternal feeling seeking an outlet in Jean.

'Jean,' wailed one of her pupils, as they turned into the school. It was the sort of school building that had been built at the turn of the century on the lines of a prison with boys, girls and infants on separate floors with iron gates all round them. A more liberal generation had tried to brighten it up with bright paint, but its days were drawing to a close. Not before time, Jean thought.

'Don't call me Jean,' she said mechanically. 'I'm Miss Young.' Miss Young for ever and ever, she thought rather sadly. She didn't really fancy a virgin life, but she could see it coming.

'My mum calls you Jean.' Mother was a neighbour and a friend. No, hardly a friend, more someone Jean had known all her life. There wasn't much time for friendship in Maggie Read's life; she had Cy and four children and that brother on her hands. As Maggie Edmondstone she had been a pretty girl, now she was plump and quiet, and still only twenty-nine, older than Jean.

'Jean, I've left my bra behind in the baths.'

'You shouldn't be wearing a bra.' Jean cast an eye on her pupil's skinny frame.

'I feel really cosy in a bra.' She scuttled round in front

to prevent her teacher getting away. 'And now I've left it behind. Can I go back and get it?'

'No, certainly not.' Jean was sharp. No girl was let out unattended these days. Not even Connie Read, who ought to be indestructible if anyone was.

'I could take Rose Allen with me.'

'Not even with Rose Allen.'

'I'd only take two minutes and it's only Scripture. No one'd notice.'

'No.'

'That's gone for good then,' said Connie in a resigned voice. 'Can't leave a thing behind in that place.'

Jean gave her a gentle push in the direction of her classroom and herself turned towards the staff room. She had a free period.

There was one woman sitting at the table by the window marking exercise books with a huge red pencil. Everyone has to have an outlet somewhere and this red pencil was Madge Cullen's. At her elbow was a big brown teapot and a tray of cups.

Jean put her hand on the teapot. 'Cold,' she said.

'I'll make some more.' Madge did not look up from her work, but went slashing on with her great red weapon.

'No, don't bother.' Jean poured out a tepid tea and drank it thirstily. It wasn't too bad. She poured another cup and lit a cigarette.

'Madge,' she said suddenly. 'Do you believe in other worlds?'

'Yes,' said Madge, and returned to her books.

'I don't mean heaven and hell and all that sort of thing. But other suns, other worlds, with other sorts of living beings on them.'

Madge was silent. 'Yes, I suppose I do. Yes, probably there are.'

54

Jean looked out of the window, upwards to the sky. 'All those galaxies, millions of them stretching farther into space than we can ever see, and each of them crowded with suns and planets. There must be people living on some of them.'

'Mm,' said Madge, studying the book before her. 'Horrible thought, isn't it?'

'But do you think they can get in touch with us?'

Madge didn't even bother to answer. She was making little moaning noises of despair over the page she was studying. 'Oh, naughty girl,' she was saying, 'oh you careless girl.'

'Could they come here and take us away, do you think?' asked Jean. She said it aloud, but Madge wasn't listening and she was glad of it. There are some things you want to shout out, but don't want anyone to hear.

She lowered her eyes from the sky with its teeming worlds to the school playground.

'What's Bernard Dodge doing mooching about out there?' she said.

'Well, he shouldn't be,' said Miss Cullen, hearing at once. 'He ought to be sitting quietly writing a nature essay on Flies. He's always where he shouldn't be.' She hurried out.

Jean watched her curiously from the window. She rather liked Bernard, who was a shy, brilliantly clever child whom no one could control. Next term he had a place at a school for specially talented children and, in Jean's opinion, even they would have to watch out. On his form Bernard was hard to match.

She saw him and his teacher stand there talking. They weren't arguing. No one argued with Bernard. You put your point and he put his and then you found yourself doing what he'd said.

Unsurprised she saw him lead Miss Cullen towards the shed where the boys kept their games equipment. He went in and she waited outside. Bernard came out carrying a bundle which he then gave to her.

Funny, funny, funny, thought Jean. What's he found?

The telephone rang on Coffin's desk. He picked it up and listened.

'What? Right. No, Headmistress, you did quite right. I'll send someone round. No, wait. I'll come myself.'

He left a message for Dove, who was out, and hurried round the corner to the school. In the entrance he found a small group made up of Jean Young, Madge Cullen, whom he'd met, and the headmistress, whom he'd known for a long time. He thought they all looked white.

'What have you got? Where did you find it? Where is it?'

'Well, I don't know,' said the headmistress. 'It may be something or it may be nothing. I couldn't be sure.'

'Let me see, then.'

'Yes. In my room.' She paused. 'One of our boys found it. I expect you'll want to see him?'

'Later. After I've seen what you've got.'

Her hand trembled as she opened her door.

'It's silly to mind so much. After all, what I'm going to show you isn't anything *human*. But sometimes inanimate objects have a character all their own.'

She looked at him pathetically, asking him to say: no, no, things don't have a life of their own. But when he looked at these he wondered if they didn't. They were laid out on her table.

There was a child's handbag of blue plastic, a scarf of blue silk, and a knife.

He looked at them and then at Miss Cullen. She shook her head.

'I don't know, but I think Miss Young might know.' She glanced at Jean Young, who was standing there white-faced. Jean nodded.

'I don't know about the scarf,' she said, 'but the handbag is Katherine Gable's. At least I think so. If it is hers you will find her initials inside written in blue ink.'

Handling the bag with a handkerchief Coffin opened it and looked inside. 'Yes, the initials K. G. are there. Where were these things found?'

The headmistress looked at Miss Cullen.

Miss Cullen cleared her throat. 'On the shed where we keep the football things,' she said; her voice came out unexpectedly loud, and she flushed.

'*On* the shed?'

'Yes. On the roof.'

'And the knife?'

'Yes, that was there too.'

Coffin turned to Jean Young. She answered his unspoken question. 'I don't think it's Katherine's. I doubt it. That's a big knife. A boy's knife.'

'It's a man's knife,' said Coffin, picking it up in his handkerchief. Then he corrected himself sadly. His eyes had caught the initials T. B. scratched on one side. 'No, only a boy's after all.' He held it to the light. 'It's just possible there might be a print there.'

He felt rotten physically; he wondered if he was going down with something.

Chapter Five

Tony Young

I feel absolutely sick about what has happened to Tom Butt. It wasn't intended, I'm sure. God, I am sorry. It means more to me than you'd think. I'm glad to get it down on this tape. It's a sort of way of speaking out silently, if you know what I mean.

Jean came in and told me about it. Of course I knew about Tom disappearing the day before. The whole street was talking about that, and Dave rang me up twice to talk to me about it and see what I thought. I didn't think much. I just felt sick. Wherever he'd gone it was a removal I didn't care to dwell upon. But, of course, they are the thoughts you find yourself thinking about most and Tom was hardly out of my thoughts all day.

I didn't know whether to feel sorry for Tom or exasperation. And that's the way it always was with him. When he was a kid at school he lived with his old grandmother and as soon as she died he moved into a hostel. His widowed mother had married an Australian and gone out to Sydney to live, leaving him behind. He said he hardly remembered her. When we were at school he'd been plump and spotty, but these last couple of years he'd cleaned himself up and was getting quite presentable. Taking it all in all, he was part of my life.

Dave thought it was a joke. 'It's like science fiction, isn't it?' he kept saying. But it was no joke. 'I wonder how they did it, eh? No one knows that, do they? No one knows and perhaps they'll never know.' That was what seemed to impress him most. I could hear admiration oozing out of him. It's dangerous to get like that.

'Things have a way of coming out,' I said sourly. 'What does Cy think?'

'Oh, Cy's not saying anything. But he's had a quarrel with my sister and he shut himself into his room and sat talking to himself for hours.'

'Oh well, keep him happy.'

'Why?'

'Because I just think life's better when Cy's happy than when he's not.'

Dave didn't know what to make of that (although what I said had the ring of truth in it), and he put the receiver down. Which was what I wanted; it was his second call that day on this subject. I'd had enough.

And then Jean came in with her news of the penknife and the kid's clothes turning up in the school playground.

'And they were on the *roof*,' she said, looking pale. 'On the roof. Just as if they'd been dropped by a bird.'

'Anyone round here got a helicopter?' I asked aloud. 'The man next door's got a new car, I know that.'

'Shut up,' she said.

'Who found it all?'

'A boy called Bernard Dodge. He's the sort that would.'

'Don't hold it against him.'

'No.' She pushed her hair back from her forehead in a way she has. 'No, I don't really. Pour me a cup of that tea.'

I gave it to her and took some more myself. It was good to taste the hot sweet drink. I had to remember that, whatever had happened to Katherine Gable and Tom Butt and the others, I was still in the body and could enjoy things of this sort. Animals like us have to take our pleasures as we find them. John Plowman was always telling us this, and for the first time it struck me as a dangerous philosophy. It hadn't been dangerous for old John, whose animal pleasures were clearly of a very restrained and moderate sort. But if someone like Cy had listened to this too much, there was no knowing what he might get up to.

'Where's Dad?'

'Out in the shed with his birds,' I said.

'Oh good.' And she nodded. What she meant was: oh good, he's safely out of the way and won't bother us. We tended to be this way about Dad and I'm afraid he begins to notice.

'Did the policeman tell you about Tom's knife being there?' I asked.

'No, of course not. But I saw it before he came. You know how good my sight is. I could read his initials. Scratched on the back of the knife, but quite easy to read.' She poured herself some more tea, drank it and then said, 'You see the significance of the knife? You see what it means?'

'Oh yes, I see,' I said. 'It means that Tom's disappearance and the children's, specifically Katherine Gable's, must have some connection.'

'It doesn't sound right, does it?' said Jean helplessly. 'I mean it just doesn't sound right. How can they be the same sort of thing?'

'There's all manner of ways.'

'You're a strange boy.'

'Thanks.'

'Sometimes you act as if you had access to knowledge no one else in the world can ever have. You're doing it now.'

'Thanks again.'

'Was Tom a friend of yours then?' she asked.

'Well, I knew him.'

I didn't go on, just poured some more hot water into the tea-pot and sat there waiting for it to brew itself into a tea of some sort. It was a worrying thought that the disappearance of the children and possibly of Tom too (and here I would have to check) coincided with dates when there had been a UFO sighting.

Some people might say it was possible they had been taken off by kidnappers from outer space.

This was the knowledge that Jean, with her good eyesight, read in my face. It was quite a thought.

It was a thought I handled with considerable reservations.

My trouble was that I associated the girl's disappearance with those noises I had on my tape. I promised to say more about those noises.

They were cries and little moans.

I made an excuse to Jean and went upstairs and looked at the tape. I didn't wish to play it. I knew well how it sounded. The beginning of the tape was a perfectly normal recording I had made myself of a concert. Well, it wasn't everyone's sort of concert. The music was Stockhausen. To me it sounded Bronze Age, heroic, stirring. The percussion went on for about ten minutes, then these other sounds started coming in. At first superimposed on the other sounds, then taking over entirely.

I was absolutely staggered when I first played the tape back and got what was on it. I could swear that when I put it away having finished recording the Stockhausen piece from the radio it was perfectly normal tape.

I had no memory at all of adding to it.

I knew that if I took the tape round to John Plowman and played it to him he'd be on to it at once and have it marked "sounds coming from out of space" before I could turn round. But God knows the noises sounded human enough to me. I thought they sounded like a child.

I picked up the tape, now neatly re-wound, and looked at it. Then I put it away. I was terrified to play it now in case Tom Butt had somehow got on it.

However, it seemed to me that I was in a very tricky position if you didn't believe, like John Plowman, in visitors from outer space and that I owed it to myself to be brave.

I played the tape. But Tom Butt had not made his entrance there. Not yet. What was there was unnerving enough, but it didn't include Tom Butt. I re-wound the tape, my machine running itself twice into trouble as I did so. I'd have to get Dave to repair it, he's a genius with machines.

I like a rational explanation for things. It may not be easy to find, but I like to think it's there. Certain facts had to be explained. First, the coincidence of the dates of a UFO sighting with the days the last two children had disappeared. Secondly, the coincidence of Tom's knife turning up with Katy Gable's possessions. Then there were these strange voices, which sounded like a child's (or children) on my tape. I didn't remember putting them there, but you could hear them. And that was what I didn't like. Looking at these things rationally it seemed to me that I had to study our Club, that I ought to dig into it really hard.

The first opportunity for digging came a few days later with our weekly Club meeting on Tuesday. It seemed an opportunity, tape, for taking you along and letting you get to know a few voices, but the chance to use you didn't arise. This is all from memory. But I've got a pretty good memory.

Judith, my ex-girl friend, was waiting outside for me that evening when I set off. At least, I deduced she was waiting because she spoke to me. Also, I don't suppose she was sitting in her car outside our house just to catch a glimpse of our lovely front garden.

'Hello,' she said.

'Hello.' I didn't like to make it too enthusiastic although I was quite pleased to see her again.

'I was just passing and I saw you come out.'

'Is that so?'

'Yes, it is just so. Don't think I was looking for you. I was just visiting an actress friend of mine who lives near here; she's married to a policeman.'

'Poor thing,' I said. I knew who she meant, of course. There's only one policeman round here married to an actress. I wish we had more of them; they make an interesting breed.

'Can I give you a lift?'

'You won't like where I'm going.' We had quarrelled, you see, about my activities in the Club. Judith didn't approve of such things. She said they made her flesh crawl, although hers was lovely flesh, crawling or otherwise. She's a beautiful girl.

'I'm trying to protect you from your future,' she said, opening the door of the car. I got in. I simply couldn't resist an opportunity to sit in it. I closed my eyes and pretended it was mine. 'If you don't watch out, if you keep going around with people like them, then you're going to end up a creepy old man.'

'That's a long way off yet,' I said comfortably.

'Then a creepy young one.'

I opened my eyes. 'Don't you think there must be something in me that agrees with what they're doing and wants to join in?' I asked seriously.

'That's where I get stuck,' she said. 'Every, every time. Want to get out and walk?'

'No.' So she drove on, her face looking sad. I felt sad myself.

'Give me time, Judith,' I said. 'Let me get this thing worked out. You never know. I might turn out to be a boy who is changing.'

She had driven me almost to John Plowman's door, but she stopped short of it. She didn't want to drive right up and I knew it.

'Well, don't change everything.' She was watching me get out of the car. 'Leave me behind something to know you by.'

I bent forward and kissed her cheek. 'When you drive away my heart goes with you,' I said.

I watched her drive away. She was a most beautiful girl and I certainly had lost my heart to that car.

Esther Glasgow was arriving just as I was and followed me up the path to John's front door. Behind her came Cy. John Plowman's wife opened the door and we all went into his sitting-room where John and a couple of other members were already waiting. Seeing them all together so soon after meeting Judith I saw them with her eyes and wondered why I stuck with them. But immediately I knew they'd never achieve anything without me and I must stay with them. A boy likes to feel he's needed.

'How's Miss Jones?' I asked John. Not having had any sort of communication from Miss Jones, either from this world or the next, I had naturally wondered.

'Oh yes, I have an announcement to make.' He cleared his throat and went and stood in front of the fireplace where he always stood to take charge of a meeting.

'Friends,' he began. He always called us friends. I think it was a hangover from some other group he must have led, probably something with a more religious flavour. 'Friends, you will be glad to know that our friend Eliza Jones has taken her operation and has stood it well.' He made it sound like an examination Miss Jones had been sitting and had satisfactorily passed. 'We have hopes of a good recovery.'

I was pleased. I liked Miss Jones. And what's more the Club needed her. She wasn't easy to fool. She had her hopes like the rest of them. She wanted to see a UFO sighting definitely established before she died, but she wouldn't settle for an easy proof. I wondered if there'd been any chance of getting anything while in hospital. This is contrary to what you'd expect; you'd expect concentrations of people, like hospitals or barracks, to get a higher average of sightings than normal. But it doesn't seem to work out that way. I suppose because in both institutions people have their heads bent towards their feet. The other suggestion is that the UFO vehicles are *shy* and don't want to be seen by lots of people. I favour this latter view myself.

John Plowman's wife brought round cups of peppermint tea and slices of oatcake. She gave me a slightly wry look as she passed me. I often wondered what she thought of it all. She never spoke, but stayed in the room with a detached look. I suppose this was why Cy Read said she was a dark soul. I think she worked as a nurse.

I read the minutes of the last meeting which were nothing, absolutely nothing at all and never were. I took care to keep the record as brief as possible.

John Plowman didn't make any little speech but asked should he sign these minutes as correct. He never did, as a rule, and usually it didn't matter. But this time it was different. Cy Read spoke up.

'You can sign them if you like, John. I wouldn't call them accurate but it makes no difference.'

'Well, thank you, Cyrus,' said John mildly. 'But I wouldn't like to do anything wrong. It's always as well to keep things straight. What's troubling you?'

Cy stood up. He walked over to place his cup on the table and then took up his position by it. I saw him catch Esther Glasgow's eye. Obviously they had it all arranged. I used to wonder sometimes if they had a great big thing going between them, but no, I don't think so. I doubt if he and Esther were even really friendly. They were just one of those temporary alliances that struggles for power always throw up.

I looked at my ally, John Plowman, and saw that he wasn't at all surprised and that he had seen it coming.

'You let the boy have too much of his own way,' said Cy, glaring at me.

I let the word "boy" go, because to someone who had Dave Edmondstone in the family a man in my age group may seem like a boy. But I took exception to the phrase about own way. I was an *administrator*. I didn't have a way of my own. I just carried out what they wanted.

'I just do what the Club wishes,' I said coldly. 'There's nothing personal about it.' Cy ignored me. That was going to be his tactics, of course. Pretend I wasn't there. Concentrate on John Plowman. Split us up.

'It was better in the old days,' went on Cy. 'When we were just a little informal group of enthusiasts. That was the way I started it.'

He put an emphasis on the phrase "I started".

'No one started it, Cy,' said John mildly. 'What we are investigating is life itself.'

'The first person in this area to try to get in touch with other workers in the field was me,' said Cy. 'At the time, if I remember, you were holding prayer meetings with that woman from Finsbury in the hope of getting in touch with astral bodies.'

'I've always maintained an interest in paranormal cognition,' said John, with a gentle smile. 'She seemed an interesting case of it.'

'She was an awful liar, that woman,' said his wife suddenly.

'My interest has always been strictly scientific,' said Cy in a loud voice, his face getting pink. 'That's how it ought to be. It's the only approach.'

'We have to keep our minds wide open,' said John, still smiling his sweet gentle smile.

'Otherwise people will think we're lunatics,' said Cy pressing right on. The flush on his cheeks had settled into an angry red patch on each cheek. His hair was wild.

I glanced round the room. Esther Glasgow was sitting there, looking fierce. Malcolm Raguzzi, who I used to think was her boy friend and now didn't, was crouching by the window wearing his crash helmet as usual. He rode a motor bike and was our scout who always went out first to check on a sighting. He usually wore his helmet; he had once spent a whole night out in the open and was afraid of frost-bite. John was wearing his green jersey suit. He always maintained that green was the universal colour and that in order to reassure any visitor from space who might arrive he ought to be dressed in green. He had found it difficult to get the exact shade he favoured in tweed, so his wife had run him up this one; it was a mite baggy round the seat. I think we looked about as normal as we ever did.

'I agree,' said Esther, her voice giving a squeak of

excitement. She put on her big blue spectacles as if the light worried her. 'We're not taken seriously.'

'I think you're a very serious girl, Esther,' I said.

'Well, I say we should abandon meeting in your house,' said Cy. 'It's got too many associations in people's minds, John. No offence, of course.'

'Oh no,' said John.

'And take a room in a building Esther knows about and make it really impersonal and businesslike.'

'We couldn't afford it. We run on a shoe string.'

'Really it would cost very little,' said Esther, giving an apologetic little cough. 'I've found out.'

'It would put us on a very firm footing,' said Cy.

– And put him effectively in charge and free him from Plowman and me. I didn't see Esther Glasgow playing much of a part once the move was over, somehow. I had never thought of Cy as a power maniac before but he was certainly showing strong signs of jealousy, possessiveness and acquisitiveness now. He was getting worse all round.

'Well now, friend Cy,' said John, putting on his most bland face, 'as you say it's a good idea, but it needs thinking about.'

He caught his wife's eye and she at once got up and came round with more peppermint tea. It was like drinking hot cough drops.

'Now,' said John, as soon as we were drinking, 'I have a report from Alvings Farm near Basingstoke (I have a very good contact there, as you may remember) of a suspected landing of a UFO one night last week in a field there. My contact gives us first news of it.'

The meeting was on. For the moment John had glossed over the rebellion. It had happened, though. We were likely to be split into two. I felt quite cheerful. I like a bit of power politics.

I wondered what would happen if I went and took my turn on the rug by the fireplace and said: And I'm watching every one of you, friends, to see if you are guilty of murder.

Afterwards, Judith was waiting for me in the car and she drove me home. I hadn't expected her, but I wasn't surprised to see her, either.

'How's your girl friend?' said Jean, as soon as I got in. She didn't miss much. She even knew what the man next door had paid for his car, which was five hundred pounds; it was a bargain.

'We're back on terms.'

'Ha!'

'No, she's a nice girl.'

'You're home early tonight.'

'Yes, it wasn't much of a meeting.'

'Breaking up?' asked Jean.

'Yes, could be. You must have second sight.'

She laughed. 'I've been watching you proceed for some years now, remember. I know how things go and how long they last. I remember when you abandoned Yoga and took up Judo. Weren't you going to be a Black Belt? I gave you twelve weeks; you lasted eleven. You may not know it, but your life is predictable. It has a pattern.'

It's at moments like this that I know why my dear Jean hasn't married yet. Any normal man would be terrified of her.

I sighed. 'Well, predict what's coming for me next.'

I was sorry as soon as I'd said this, because then I remembered my tape. Sometimes what's coming is what you don't want and don't expect.

Chapter Six

What you didn't want and what you didn't expect were so inextricably a part of John Coffin's life that he had long since taken them for granted.

But even he was sometimes, it was inevitable, taken by surprise. He was surprised that morning when Dove came in and said he'd got his car back. Not because he'd got the car back – stolen cars were often retrieved – but because it was back unharmed.

'Yes, not even scratched either,' Dove said.

'Where was it?'

'Parked in the road just beyond the Blue Anchor. No one saw it parked there, but the man on his beat next morning recognized it. I've had a good look over it and I'd say it had even been polished.'

'Well, that's good.'

'I'd like to know who'd had it though,' said Dove. 'Know what they left inside? A rubber duck. A kid's rubber duck.'

'A family man,' said Coffin. 'You can keep the duck.'

'Yes.' Dove looked awkward, then he said, 'At first I thought it might be someone having some sort of joke on my name. You know, Dove, Duck. But no, I don't think so. It's an old duck. You can see the child loved this duck – there's a ring of dirt round the neck where it was hugged. So now I feel sorry for the kid that's lost the duck.'

'Someone's lost a duck and we've found a knife.'

'Yes, that's what I've come about. It's definitely Butt's.

As well as the initials, the fingerprints checked with those on the case in his room at the hostel.'

'Yes. Oh I remember the case. I thought you'd find a print there. He obviously kept everything he had in that case.'

'It was about the only place you could keep anything in.'

They were both silent, remembering their inspection of the room where Tom Butt had lived. When they had gone round it was already obvious he was never going to come back to it. His few possessions were still scattered about it, but already they looked forlorn. A case had been under the bed, locked. Inside was little except a few cheap clothes, a bundle of letters and a soft grey felt hat of a type no longer worn.

'I think he inherited it,' said Dove, taking it out and looking at it. 'I can remember my uncle wearing hats like this, but it's a long, long while since I've seen one close to. Someone gave it to him and it was too good to throw away so he kept it.'

'Yes, perhaps you're right.' Coffin was walking round the room, which was tiny and contained little except a bed and a small locker painted white, but in this Tom seemed to have kept nothing at all.

'He didn't like the locker,' said the housekeeper, who was with them. 'I don't think he trusted it. Or anyone really.'

'And how right he was,' said Coffin.

'You don't think he'll come back?'

Coffin shook his head. He didn't think so. 'A pity he didn't have friends. Or someone to talk to. No one seemed to talk to him. Have you noticed that?'

'He was a bit locked up inside. Not his fault, of course.

He wasn't the sort that was going to settle down and be happy. He wasn't happy.'

As long as that's all, thought Coffin. Because now that Tom's knife had turned up with the missing Katherine Gable's possessions, he had to ask himself if Tom hadn't known something about the disappearance of the girl.

'How long has he been living here?'

'Not long. About three months. Since March.'

Two of the missing girls had disappeared since March. Of course, another had disappeared the year previously, but it had always been a possibility that this case was separate from the other two.

'In that case we have two abductors to look for,' pointed out Dove sadly.

'That's always been on the cards.'

The room was shut and locked and presently it would be photographed and searched for fingerprints.

The result of this fingerprinting they now had before them.

'Well, I always did think the knife was his,' said Coffin, looking now at the matched prints in a photograph in front of him. 'But a lot of what we make of it depends on when he last had it on him.'

Because if Tom Butt had lost it then the link between him and Katherine Gable was broken.

'All his mates have been questioned about the knife. No one remembers if he had it the day he went.'

'It was a strange business, the day he went,' said Coffin suddenly. 'You know, I don't quite believe in it.'

'I never have. But try finding something to put in its place.'

Coffin considered. 'And what about the girl's bag and scarf? Nothing to help there?'

'They are hers, of course. I had to get the mother to identify them.' He blinked, not enjoying the memory.

'You know what,' said Coffin, getting up. 'I'm going to see the men on the building site again.' He looked out of the window.

'They won't be pleased,' said Dove. 'They work on a type of piece rate system round there. Bonuses and so on. Every minute spent talking to you and me is worth money to them.'

But the boy who had heard the original call for help and to whom they spoke first was quite willing to talk at length. He found his work there boring and was considering leaving it.

'Start from the beginning,' said Coffin.

'Well, the buzzer went and I picked up the telephone and I heard Tom asking for help. I didn't catch the first few words, in fact I didn't know what he was saying. It's not good, that line. Then it came loud and clear. I can't remember the exact words now, but it was what I told you the first time.'

'I can read it to you: he called out "Help me, help me, they're getting me." Then he said "the power's gone" and then he called "Help Help," again.'

'Yes, that was how it was.'

'But he never said who he was, never named himself,' pointed out Coffin.

'No, I suppose not.'

'Did you recognize his voice?'

'That line's bad. Still, it was Tom, wasn't it? We found his clothes.'

'That was a funny thing too,' said Coffin.

'Well, I suppose he must have been up there.'

'You convinced about that?' said Coffin.

The boy looked at him and muttered something inaudible. They let him go. Then they saw the foreman and the two other men who had been in the forefront of the group that night. Each man repeated the story he had told before. But at each telling the effect seemed to shrink more and more and Tom's figure to become fainter.

They had the boy back again.

'After you'd taken the call and were getting help and had come back to look at the cage, could you then see Tom Butt standing up there?'

'Well, I suppose so.'

'But you couldn't really see much, could you?'

'You're muddling me,' said the boy. 'What do you want me to say? I'm doing the best I can.'

'What's your best?' said Coffin to Dove when the boy had left.

'That Tom wasn't there at all.'

'Yes, that's mine too. There was a woman too, wasn't there? Where is she? Not disappeared too?'

'No.' Dove consulted a list. 'She's called Mrs Nancy Rogers and lives in Peel Terrace. But she wouldn't be there now, she works in the school, helps serve the lunches. She'll be there now.'

Mrs Rogers was laying a long trestle table with a set of knives and forks and spoons. Down the row she went, knife, fork, spoon, gap, then knife, fork and spoon again. She was along one side and had started up the other before they could stop her.

In fact, they didn't stop her. 'Yes, what is it now?' she said, still moving. 'I suppose I know, though.'

Now that Coffin looked at her properly he saw that she had a pleasant, good-humoured face.

'This is the slow table I'm doing,' she informed them.

'Slow eaters?'

74

She gave a hoot of laughter. 'No. Slow at everything else. Slow readers, slow workers, slow minds. They can eat as fast as anyone else, though. Well, go on, tell me what you want.'

For a moment she stood still and waited for them, her eyes vague and unfocused.

'When you stood below the cage and looked up, what could you see?'

'He was standing there in one corner.'

Coffin nodded. 'And you heard him call out?'

'I thought I did then. I'm not so sure now. Things fade.'

'Of course they do.'

'And is that all you wanted?' she said ironically.

'For the moment.'

'Two of you to ask that! I'll get back to work, then.'

'I think you've left a gap down there at the bottom,' said Coffin nodding towards the end of the table.

'What?' She peered forward, and was halfway down the room before she stopped. 'No. No, all complete. You want your eyes tested.'

'She never really saw much at all, did she?' asked Dove, as they left.

'No. She can hardly see to the end of the room, let alone halfway up a building.'

'She didn't see anything; we didn't see anything; they didn't see anything.'

'He wasn't there,' said Coffin. 'He worked some trick with the phone. For some reason he wanted out.'

'What a way to go.'

'Not if he'd kidnapped and murdered two children already. It might be quite a good idea.'

'Yes.'

They walked slowly back to the station.

'Funny, he didn't sound that sort,' said Dove.

'Oh well, it's never quite how you think it is,' said Coffin. 'Let's try and get him. Get the machine rolling. And it might be worth going to see that girl again. The one who came back.'

So the machine started rolling and descriptions of Tom Butt were sent out to all stations. No one had a photograph of him so they made up a composite picture of him, which was not very like, but which appeared in the press and on the television screen.

Meanwhile Dove went out and interviewed the girl who had disappeared for a few hours and then come back. When previously questioned she had simply said she'd got lost. She had been so silent that among the police who'd questioned her she was known as the Silent Girl. No one had been sure if she really had something to tell or was silent because she had indeed just got lost.

Now Dove could ask her about Tom Butt.

A stone's throw from where Coffin was working was an old building which had been a livery stables some fifty years ago and probably had a history even older than that. It had a cobbled courtyard around which were the boxes where the horses had lived. It had housed a taxi service and for the last ten years had been let out as garages. Now even this usage was coming to an end and it had been bought for the value of the site, which was not inconsiderable. The new owner, Mr Di Finzio, was having a look round.

He was going round it with his assistant, who was reluctant and nervous.

'Terrible job they made when they put doors on these old horse boxes,' he said, giving one a kick. He had started life as a carpenter in a circus and knew what to look for.

76

'It was done just after the war when they didn't have the timber.'

'Well, it'll all go now. This whole area is going to be rebuilt.' He sounded gleeful. 'Dunno how it hung on so long. Wouldn't have done, either, but for some bit of trouble about the land title. Bit of luck for me, though.' He kicked at another spintering door. 'This is where I make my fortune.'

'Yes,' said his assistant, who was poorly paid.

'What's in here?' Di Finzio said, giving the door yet another blow. 'You checked on everything like I told you?' He had owned the place a few weeks now, but this was his first look round.

'I've been over everything. That's a sort of storage place. Must have been let out as that some time.'

'Well, it ought to have been cleared out.'

The assistant shrugged. 'I suppose it wasn't worth anyone's while. Anyway, there's nothing valuable there, I can tell you that. If there had been it would have gone.'

'Anyone could get in here.'

'Can't keep 'em out.'

They were progressing, slowly and inevitably, towards a certain point. The broken door had swung open, revealing the remains of packing cases and straw.

'What's that smell?'

'I don't smell anything.'

The new owner sniffed. 'Perhaps I imagined it. Oh well, what's it matter, it'll all be gone soon.' He moved away. 'Let's get out of here. To tell you the truth, I don't like it so much. Know what I was during the war? I was a Heavy Demolition Worker. *You* won't know what that was. Who cares now? And that's how I smelt smells like that . . . ' He stopped uneasily.

'There can't be anything here.'

'No. What's in that packing case? You looked?'

'Not in that one, no.'

'You'll have to be more thorough than that, boy, if you're going to make your fortune. Look now.'

The top of the packing case was covered with an old sack. Underneath that shavings. And underneath that . . .

'Gawd!' said the new owner, forgetting the new language he was learning to go with his new home and his new car and his success. To his horror he felt violently sick and began to tremble. 'I didn't imagine that smell then. Cover him up. Where's the 'phone?' He stumbled off.

Tom Butt had come rushing back into everyone's life. The speed of his arrival increased when they discovered how he had died.

'So what's it all about?' asked Dove. He had seen the Silent Girl, who was still silent. 'Is it suicide or murder? Well, which is it? Did he kill himself?'

'He didn't put himself where he was found,' said Coffin. 'Or cover himself up. So it could be murder.'

But there was a strange note in his voice and Dove waited.

'And you've got to remember he had no clothes on. We ought to have expected that, as we found his clothes in the cage.' Dove still waited.

'On the other hand, he could have killed himself,' went on Coffin.

'How?'

Coffin got up and looked out of the window at the building site. 'Here's the news. Every bone in his body seems to have been broken. It looks as though he fell from a great height.'

Chapter Seven

Tony Young

So then the news about Tom got around and we all heard it as we came home from work. I felt really sick. And I rushed up here to my tape and poured out all I knew, which wasn't much. I may have set the wrong tone in talking about Tom Butt, may have let you get sorry for him beyond what he deserved. We were bad to Butty. Yes, all right. But that wasn't the end of it.

For Butty hadn't stayed still. His character, in case I haven't made it clear, developed. From being a cowed fat boy with a touch of colour (yes, there was that too) he became an aggressive fat boy. One day he rounded on us. We were doing something vaguely hostile to him. I can't remember what, when, stimulated I suppose by all the glands that dominate a boy's life, he kicked our shins and bashed our surprised noses. He had great beefy hands so the blows were heavy. One of us (not me) cried. Then he grabbed someone's schoolbag and books and threw them up on the roof of the old shed where we kept our football boots. We couldn't get them down and the boy who had to go home without his luggage got beaten.

We left Butty alone after that. In fact, I think it was then that Dave took over as scapegoat and was put in Butty's place.

What I didn't like was the way Tom had gone. I didn't think the birds had picked him up and then dropped him down from a great height, but it happened somehow. And if I didn't like the way he had gone, even less did I like the way he had come back. Or, to put it differently, where he had been found. I didn't know what the police made of it, but the police didn't have my sources of information.

I really poured out my heart on that tape, being very careful not to put too much too clearly. Who can say who could hear what? After all, once a thing's been put into speech you can never keep it quiet, however discreet you think you've been. The police thought none of us knew the nature of Tom's injuries, but we did. Of course we did.

From next door I could hear the Lees kid crying. He'd been at it all day. It was really beginning to worry me. I stumped down to the kitchen and asked Jean what it was all about.

She shrugged. 'He's lost something, I think.'

'Haven't we all?'

'It upsets him.'

'I can hear it.'

I could hear his father's voice as well. He too seemed upset.

'Has *he* lost something?' I asked. But Jean didn't answer.

Then I went upstairs again. I thought I'd just check up on the tape with the strange noises. There might be something there to help me.

I put it on, sound very low. I waited. At first I thought I'd got it too low, because I couldn't hear anything. So I turned the sound up. I ran the whole reel through.

But there was nothing. Nothing at all. The tape had been wiped clean. Old Mother Hubbard went to the cupboard, and when she got there the cupboard was bare. That was how I felt.

I stumped downstairs to the kitchen where Jean was working. I sat down at the table and drank some bitter tea. I wasn't unhappy, but I wasn't exactly happy either. More unsettled in my mind. To be honest I was considering if I'd gone mad. Or perhaps had been mad for some time.

Jean was pleased to see me. 'You know I think he *has* lost something,' she said in an excited tone.

'Who has?'

'Mr Lees next door.' She sounded pleased and interested. I could see she was enjoying the small mystery. 'I'm sure he has. I can tell from his voice.'

I wondered if she could tell from my voice what I'd lost. I was beginning to think it was my reason that was gone.

'And I think I know what it was,' she said triumphantly.

I didn't answer, so she prodded me a little. 'Haven't you noticed something that's missing?'

'I'm not good at noticing something that isn't there.' Which was a lie: I was sharp on noticing something that wasn't there. Like the noises that had been on my tape.

'His car,' she said. 'His car's gone.'

'Perhaps he's sold it.' I didn't care much. I cared about the girl in the white Triumph and I cared about Tom Butt.

'No! He's only just bought it. No, the car's been stolen. I bet that's it. And perhaps the child left something in it and lost that too.'

I let her go on with it. I could see her deductions were taking her mind off our real mystery, what was really missing round here.

So Tom was dead. I hadn't wanted him dead. But now I had to decide if I was in any way responsible.

Chapter Eight

The premises where Tom Butt had been found were closed up and a policeman put on duty. The police were not finished with it but for the moment there was a lull. They had no idea yet who was responsible for putting him there. 'We've had a good look round and done all the usual, but nothing obvious has come up,' said Dove to Coffin.

'No, there wouldn't be. All that straw and dirt.'

'Yes. We found an old bridle that must have been there thirty years at least. But the body hadn't been there for long.'

'You don't think so?'

'I know so.'

'Come on, then, tell me.'

'Well, he was the wrong shape. He didn't fit into that box. Someone had a job shoving him in. He'd already stiffened.'

'Yes,' said Coffin reflectively. 'I saw that. And the pathologist?'

'Confirms it. I had the report through. He hasn't had time to do much, but as we thought, he died from injuries due to a fall.'

'Someone dropped him or he was pushed.'

'Or he jumped,' said Dove, giving his superior a sharp look. 'It still could be a suicide.' He thought his superior was moving on too rapidly.

Then he said: 'But the real thing is, do we treat it as

part of the missing girls business or as something out on its own?'

'It's connected,' said Coffin. 'Where's the knife? It's connected all right and we didn't do the connecting.'

He caught sight of Dove's expression. 'And don't think I'm not bearing that in mind. Someone could have put the knife there just for us to make a connection.'

'I love that thought,' said Dove. 'It gives just one more complication to add up.'

'And it already adds up,' said Coffin. 'We have three missing girls. We have Tom Butt's knife which turned up with some possessions of one of the girls. And now we have the dead body of Tom Butt himself.'

'I'd like to believe it was suicide,' said Dove wistfully. 'That might wrap it up. Butt kills the kids and then kills himself.'

'He didn't bury himself.'

'Nothing's impossible,' said Dove who knew that anything could happen and that once you knew how, it looked easy.

'There's one thing I'm going to do,' said Coffin vindictively. 'I'm going to tear apart that garage where Tom Butt was found, to see what is there.'

'I'm rather short of men,' said Dove apprehensively.

'Then borrow. But go over it with a toothcomb.'

In the old stables now a garage there were a dozen old loose boxes grouped round a central cobbled yard with a drain in the middle. Over the stables ran a huge loft where the grooms had once slept. Bits of it were partitioned off. All of it was full of lumber.

'It's going to take a lot of time,' said Dove.

Time gallops for children when they are playing. When they are imagining something, it disappears altogether.

Belle Anderson had a watch, but as she never wound it up, it had stopped permanently at three o'clock. Belle didn't mind. Inside her was her own particular clock which told her all the time she needed to know and which by no means marched with Greenwich Mean Time.

Belle was very pretty. She had thick curly hair, bright eyes and a clear skin. She was a little plump, with a hint of future stockiness; this didn't matter now, but perhaps when she was adult she would not be quite so pretty.

To be a ten-year-old girl child, to be dreamy, and to be prettier now than you will ever be again makes a dangerous combination.

Without being able to put it into words her mother was aware of it and was uneasy.

'Where have you been all this time, Belle? You're late,' she said as her daughter came in from school.

'Out playing.' Her daughter gave her a radiant smile.

'I know that. Playing what?'

'Games.'

'Who with?'

'The man from the moon.'

'Don't talk nonsense, Belle.'

Belle was silent, but gave her mother her sweet, secretive smile.

'I know girls like to play imaginative games, Belle, but you mustn't say that sort of thing. It's practically telling a lie.'

'Well, perhaps not the moon. I don't know that it is the moon. I just thought the moon. But from somewhere far away.' Her face became dreamy.

'Oh, Belle.'

'I don't believe in fairies, mother.' Belle looked amused. 'I know what's real.'

Her mother swallowed the exasperation her daughter

frequently aroused in her. She knew that Belle had her own idea of reality and that it was no good banging your head against it. She had been a great romancer in her own youth, often getting punished for "telling lies". (*Her* mother had not hesitated to use that word.) Adult herself now, she saw her own child's dilemma. You did tell the truth, but the words you used sounded different to those outside your dream world.

'Well, you shouldn't go off on your own,' she said, getting down to what really worried her.

'Oh, I wasn't alone,' said Belle. 'There were ever so many of us. Hundreds and hundreds.'

'And where were these hundreds? I don't know any place round here big enough to hold hundreds of you,' said her mother in a sharp voice.

'Not big,' said Belle. 'Tiny, tiny.'

'I ought to shake you.'

'Yes, mother. I'm just packing up my things.' For the last few weeks she had been treasuring a tiny toy plastic suitcase. 'You see I brought some of the little things back with me and I'm putting them in my case.'

'Treasures from the moon, I suppose.'

'Yes, mother. If it's the moon.'

'Oh, it's the moon, all right. We don't believe in dreams, you and me.'

'They are real things, mother. I'll just put my little things away.' She opened her suitcase, pale blue with a dog painted on it. As far as her mother could see, it was empty except for a pink silk scarf. 'Now mind, Belle,' she said, 'Don't go wandering out by yourself again. Never mind the hundreds and hundreds of others. Just don't go out by yourself.'

'No, mother.'

It was a lovely evening.

'Go and play in the garden.'

'Yes, mother.'

The house had a small but pretty garden with a shed and an apple tree in it. Even though it was London, apples grew on this tree in season. The family had one other child, a small boy, and an aged mongrel dog.

The boy and the dog were in the garden too.

Belle went out and stood near the apple tree. After a while the boy went and joined her. The dog stayed where he was, which was lying in the shade near the house. He was getting old and only moved around now when he had to.

Belle's mother went inside and finished sewing a cotton dress she was making for herself. Then she pressed it with a warm iron, then she hung it up to admire it. Then she walked over to the kitchen window to see where the children were, Belle, aged ten, and the boy, Jim, aged three. He was rather a slow three-year-old and not much of a talker yet.

When she had put the dress away in a cupboard and tidied the room, she looked out of the window again. The children were not to be seen. There was the garden, there was the tree and there was Sam, the dog. Sam hadn't moved, hadn't been disturbed. Fancy, she thought, I don't remember Belle having a pink silk scarf.

'Sam,' she called. 'Where are the children?'

Sam looked at her and then looked at the end of the garden as if he could see them clearly.

From the window, she called 'Belle, Belle, where are you?' But there was no answering cry.

She stumbled back into the kitchen, into the arms of her husband who had just come in.

'I've lost the children,' she said. 'They've gone. They're not in the garden.'

He looked at her in surprise and then looked over her shoulder into the garden.

'Lost them?' he said. Gently he turned her round to face the window.

Through it she could see Belle and Jim, hand in hand, coming up the path. Belle was carrying her little suitcase.

'Belle, where were you?'

'We were right there all the time, Mummy. Couldn't you see us?'

'No, I could not see you.'

'We were there,' said Belle again. 'Behind the tree.'

'Why didn't you answer when I called?'

'We came, Mummy,' said Belle.

The episode still rankled with their mother even after the children were in bed.

'I could have sworn they weren't there.'

'They were there,' said her husband awkwardly. He hated to get into arguments between his wife and his children. He had a strong feeling that in such a situation he could only lose.

'I didn't see them.'

'That's just it: you didn't see them.'

'I didn't see them, but they were there?' She sighed. 'Well, I suppose so.'

They sat for a while in silence and he read his evening paper. Then she said suddenly, 'She's playing some kind of a game with me.'

'Who is?'

'Belle. She was playing with me.'

'She's a bit young to do that.'

'Oh no, she's not.'

She went to the bottom of the stairs and listened quietly. 'Still asleep.'

'What did you expect?'

'I don't know what I expected.' She came back wearily. 'All right. They were there all the time and I didn't see them. Where do people go when one can't see them?'

It wasn't a question to be answered and he didn't try to answer it. 'Come on back and sit down and leave it alone. Next time you can't see them don't decide you've lost them.'

'Perhaps you're right.' She came back and sat down.

'It's good advice. Take my word for it.'

So the next sunny evening when the children went out to play, Belle and her brother together, their mother did not worry when she could not see them in the garden. A little later she looked in the street, but making it a casual glance, without too much anxiety.

She couldn't see them, but after all, they must be there. She had her husband's word for it.

By the time they were reported missing it was late evening.

'Four hours ago she noticed they weren't around. Four hours before we were let know,' said Coffin angrily. 'Who's responsible for this?'

'The husband and wife about equally between them,' said Dove. 'But the children may turn up, of course.' He didn't sound hopeful.

'Well, it clears Tom Butt. Whoever's responsible, he's not.'

'Any news there?'

'About three tubs full of rubbish left behind by previous tenants of the garage, but nothing much about Tom. He's still our problem, he hasn't solved anything for us.'

'No, I never thought he had.'

Coffin went over to his window and looked down Saxe-Coburg Street. He often stood there thinking and had no idea that his figure silently looming there was in itself one of the sights of Saxe-Coburg Street.

'Crazy business,' he said aloud. 'You realize that, don't you? Tom didn't disappear from that lift, he was never in it, he was probably already dead.'

'I know that.'

'But someone rigged up that business, spoke to that other lad on the 'phone, pretended to be Tom, thought it worth while to get up a charade. That's crazy. But you and I have to take the fantasy out and put it back on its feet.'

'It's not normal, no.'

'But we've got to make it normal. Or no, we can't quite do that, but we've got to find out what is real and rational about it. Why it happened just the way it did.'

'I'd like to be around the time we ever do that,' said Dove.

'And it's coming from out there.' Coffin tapped on his window. 'Some boy out there knows plenty. And some woman knows he knows plenty and isn't saying.'

When Tony Young heard the news about the children, which he heard as soon as he came in from his work on the evening of the day following, he at once rushed upstairs and put the tape on his recorder and played it back.

No, there were no noises. No new noises, which was what he had feared.

He came downstairs.

'Where was I last night, Jean?' he asked.

'Where were you?' She looked surprised. 'Well, you were out for a bit. You went round to see John Plowman but he'd gone out on one of his trips and you came back.'

'I wasn't gone long, was I?'

'No, you were back sooner than I expected.'

'Expected, Jean?'

'Yes. Usually when John goes off on one of these trips you're gone a long time.'

'But this time I was back soon?'

'Yes.'

'That's right, Jean,' said Tony. 'That's how it was and you stick to it. I'll be all right as long as you do that.'

He shuddered.

Chapter Nine

Tony Young

It came out of my heart, that shudder did, out of my heart and went right down to my boots. I'm a sensitive boy and I felt that shudder so that it hurt. Misery is a city, and I was on the outskirts walking in.

That evening the police called. Not on me specially, they were simply making a house to house check on all houses with men in them. They wanted to know where Dad and I had been on the previous evening. Dad was easy: he'd been with his birds and a bird watcher friend had been in his company. But no one had ever seriously considered that Dad had any interest outside his birds. With me it was more difficult. I'd been out and then I'd been in, but there were certainly gaps in my evening when I was unattended. I could see this particular policeman give me an appraising look and I knew what it meant. Was I or was I not a likely candidate for murder?

I suppose I didn't look too happy, my shudder was still sitting inside me ready to break out again, and he gave me another long observant look. He was a tall, plump young man, about twice my size. I wasn't the only one he was looking at. In a quiet way he was studying my sister as well. Jean too was interested. Not everyone would have known it, but I knew it. I would have been happy to see her married. But perhaps not to a policeman. All this time I had been bringing home thin mates for her to get to know and what she had been looking for was a plump policeman. Then too he had a faint reddish tinge to his hair and this may have appealed to her. I remembered that our old dog was a golden-coloured spaniel and she'd always been very fond of him.

'Would you be willing to let the police take your fingerprints if necessary?' he asked me politely.

'No. That is, under certain circumstances the answer would be yes. But at the moment it is no.'

'And what would those circumstances be?' he asked smoothly.

'That you had a fingerprint to check them against. But you haven't, have you? You haven't found anything, even a child.'

'We may have done,' he said in a noncommittal way.

'No. You couldn't keep it quiet. In some districts, yes. But not here. We all live too close together.'

'I'll just put down that you prefer not to be finger-printed, shall I?' he said.

'You would be willing, wouldn't you, Tony?' put in Jean; she looked shocked.

'No. I don't want them just bearing away my prints. I don't know what they'd do with them. Be reasonable, Jean. I'm not being objective or anything. I just have a feeling that I'd like to keep my fingerprints to myself. Unless it's absolutely necessary, which it isn't.'

'As a matter of fact, I didn't ask for it,' said the policeman.

'No. You just wanted to see how I reacted. Well, I have reacted.'

Jean showed him out. When she came back, although she was still mad with me (showing off, she muttered) she was pleased deep down inside. She liked him. Well, let him like her too, if he could.

'I'm going out, Jean,' I said.

'What?'

'Out.' I was putting on my coat. In the evening I

usually sit around in jeans and a cotton shirt. 'You've got Dad to look after you.'

'I wasn't thinking about being looked after,' she said furiously.

'What did that policeman say to you as he went out?'

'He said to tell you not to be foolish.'

I weighed it up. 'No, he never said that. That's the school-marm in you coming out, Jean.'

I bet he'd said something, though, and it was probably on the lines of 'Can we not meet again sometime, Miss Young? Surely we were at school (or Sunday School) together?' He was perfectly neutral about me, but I was not neutral about him.

I walked pretty slowly, because I wanted to think. Remember what I said about there being other factors in the disappearance of the children? I said: with these child crimes it's nearly always someone they know. This is what gets them off their guard. But there are other factors.

I went over things once again in my own mind. Five children had disappeared. Shirley Boyle was the first to go. Then Grace Parker in April. Then Katherine Gable. Now two others, Belle Anderson and her brother, both known to me. I knew all their names. They knew mine.

From the way the children had disappeared I thought (and I was not alone in thinking this) that it looked as though they must have known the man who took them away.

But it went further than that. I thought the children had co-operated. I suppose I'd better explain what I mean. It seemed to me that these missing children must have held out a helping hand to the person who wanted to carry them away. Maybe this was over-stating it. Perhaps they hadn't actually helped in their own abduction but they must have been willing.

Willing or merely docile?

What makes a child docile? None of the young inhabitants of this quarter were docile by nature. From what I remembered of my schooldays we were a rough, aggressive lot. The girls were as bad as the boys, if not worse.

So I was considering how these suspicious kids could have been made so docile.

But, come to think of it, adults can be docile too. Weren't we, in our circle of UFO watchers, an easily led little group? I often wondered, to tell you the truth, how John Plowman managed over his "sighting". He had some mixture of personal magnetism and persuasion that operated on the minds of some of our group. They believed what he wanted them to believe. Whether he believed himself I am not quite sure. I think he did and that was his strength.

Once or twice I had thought maybe he had some drug he used, something he slipped in that tea his wife handed out. I never took it myself. If I accepted a cup to look easy I slipped the drink in her azalea plant. I noticed that plant never flourished.

I suppose I'm making John out to be a pretty complicated character, but the truth is, I think he was.

It seemed to me there was a choice. Once you accepted that it was no coincidence that the children disappeared on days when a little group of us were out checking on a reported UFO sighting, then either you believed the kids had gone into outer space on a flying saucer, or you believed one of us had the responsibility.

I knew which I believed. To begin with, we've never had any sightings of UFOs over Saxe-Coburg Street.

That brought it down to a select little group: John Plowman, Miss Jones, Esther Glasgow and Cyrus. There were one or two other possibilities, such as Esther Glasgow's boy friend, but the ones I named are those who most often went out on night expeditions with John and had been out on the nights in question. They weren't all out on all the relevant dates, but most of them had been out on most of them. And of course John always had been. There was a certain sick little thought in my mind connected with Tom Butt, but I didn't want to go into this now.

It was always on an evening the children went. I wondered if I could make that mean anything. Tom, however, was different.

Anyway I thought I'd go round and go over our Club papers (we have a little shed in John's garden I use as an office) and see what I could find. On the way round I picked up Dave. Or he picked me up. I think he was on the look out for me. I had a passing wistful thought about Judith and her car, but I didn't think she'd be back. Perhaps we would meet one day when we were old, old people and spare a smile for what might have been. Or more likely, be glad we'd given each other a miss. Dave was surrounded by the crowd of little kids he always seemed to have with him. At a close look most of them were his sister's brood. He shook them off and came to walk beside me.

'I was waiting for you.'

'Yes.' I nodded. 'I'm going on business, Dave.'

'Can't I come?' He always said it like that, like a child.

'I suppose so. Keep quiet, though, and don't touch.'

'I'm never much of a talker, Tony.'

'You talk to me a lot.'

'Yes, only to you. Not to my sister. Can't talk to her.'

'And Cy?'

'I *watch* Cy.'

'That's enough, I should think. How's the job?' He had a new job. But he was always getting new jobs. To tell you the truth, so was I. I worked on a roundabout at the fairground once, enjoyed it too. Sometimes Dave and I followed each other in jobs. 'What is it this time?'

'It's something in the city.' He was a terrible liar in a fluent kind of way. You could never believe him, but it was difficult to fault him. He wasn't at all clever either; it was just a gift.

'Banking, I suppose?'

He looked solemn. Perhaps it *was* banking.

I could guess from the shut-up look of his house that both John and his wife were out. I knew they had plenty of outside activities. There was a faith healer they were rather devoted to out in Ealing and they might be there: John's rheumatism had been bad lately.

I let myself into the shed with David silently behind me. He was breathing exceptionally heavily, though, which I knew meant extreme interest.

I went over to the cupboard where I kept my papers and pretended to sort through them. I'd never let Dave in here before and he couldn't keep his hands off anything. I knew how it would be, he's like a child.

'Don't touch,' I said, shuffling through a pile of correspondence we'd had about a woman who came down from Venus to call on a housewife in the Essex marshes. She'd had pale golden hair and intense eyes. I thought she sounded a find, but she was never likely to call on me.

'Pictures,' said Dave.

'Yes, we have pictures.'

Having got Dave happily sorting over pictures of the Flying Saucer that landed in a field in Buckinghamshire one day last April, I went on to what I really wanted. (Well, they weren't actually pictures of the Flying Saucer, but you could see the hollow where it had landed, denting the ground, and a bare patch where it had burnt the grass. There was also a large and helpless looking sheep in the picture, but I don't suppose that had anything to do with it.) I went over to the set of drawers which John reserved for himself and tried to open them. I knew they were locked. I tried one after another, but it wasn't going to be easy to get one open.

'Here, let me,' said Dave, abandoning his pictures and coming over. A locked drawer was something that really got him excited. He tested a drawer. 'I couldn't see anything in those pictures. Was I missing anything?'

'You might be.' I had sometimes wondered if I was missing things in these pictures, because I never seemed to see what the others saw, not even as much as Miss Jones, who was so honest. They all looked like normal country scenes to me. I never seemed to see the signs of where a saucer had landed.

Dave produced a metal rod from his pocket, slid it into the lock, fiddled with it for a moment and then gave me a broad smile.

'There you are.'

'You're wasted in that bank.' I pulled open the drawer, only to find nothing but a few boxes of letters. I would have liked to read them through, as they looked promising: the first one was addressed to "Dear Earth Brother". But there wasn't time, and they weren't what I was looking for. Maybe I could come back here later.

'Can you shut this up again so that it won't show we opened it?'

'Sure.' Dave performed his magic again, and I thought what a dangerous person he was to have around.

The next drawer had nothing much either except a length of muslin that I thought might have played a basic part in one of John's productions. I knew he had once been important in the spirit world and had received a visit from Mr D. D. Home. You wouldn't think dead mediums would drop in on other mediums, would you? But I suppose it's a sort of inspection, and they have to see that standards are kept up.

But the third drawer had the right sort of smell and I knew straight away that I had got what I wanted. I think John must have been a herbalist in one manifestation or another. Here were neatly packaged transparent envelopes of herbs. Some were undoubtedly the makings for the herb tea we drank. I knew his wife grew and dried her own herbs. But as well as these I found a box of other dried leaves. I smelt them. They just smelt of bay. But I did wonder if a few of these infused with our peppermint tea might not have an interesting effect.

I put some of the dried leaf on my tongue and sucked; I gave some to Dave. It tasted peppery and my tongue felt first hot, then thick as if I'd bitten it.

'Here, Dave,' I said hurriedly. 'Spit it out before it gets dangerous.'

'No, I like it.' He sounded dreamy.

'Shut the drawer, then, before we pass out on the spot.'

'Right.' We both seemed to be sitting on the floor, but he heaved himself up, shut the drawer and then sank back.

'You know my new girl friend,' said Dave, turning towards me.

'Yes.'

'She's wonderful. The best yet. I wish you could meet her.'

'You never let me.'

'I feel funny about it.'

'Try me.'

'You might laugh,' he said shyly.

I felt awful, as if I really had treated him terribly when he said that.

'Tell me, Dave,' I said. 'Is it my fault? Have I destroyed your confidence?'

He looked at me as if he didn't understand what I meant. I'm not sure if I did either. We were sitting there with our backs to the wall when John Plowman walked in on us.

He gave me a sideways look. I suppose I looked pretty dopey sitting there. I stood up. Then I saw he was not alone.

'This is Mr Jasna, who has just flown in from Sagitarius,' he said, introducing us politely. 'Sagittarius in the Inner Galaxy.'

'Hello,' said Mr Jasna. He was a tall thin person with almost no hair; he wore a tight-fitting suit of some green material. No buttons were discernible but something like a zip up the front.

'Flown?' I said.

'You call it flying,' said Mr Jasna. 'It's a loose term for what I did. Not true flying. It's a sort of superphysical projection.'

'He talks English,' said Dave.

'I studied it before I came on my trip,' said Mr Jasna modestly. He had studied a slight cockney accent too.

John Plowman was looking at him with pride, rather like someone who has at last caught that rare spotted tiger he was looking for.

'I have come on a mission, of course,' said Mr Jasna.

'How did you happen to meet up with John?' I asked. But I didn't really need to ask. I knew the answer. There's a sort of built-in communication system between John Plowman and space-men missionaries like Mr Jasna. It must be a kind of radar system like some insects have, I believe. Perhaps they scent each other.

'Mr Jasna wanted to look round,' said John Plowman.

'Naturally I am interested,' said Mr Jasna. 'This place has been known to us by its intense wave activity for so many years. Now I see it.'

'That must make a difference,' I said. 'Is it what you expected?'

'Of course I'd had a very good radio picture of it before I set out. I knew what to expect. Seeing is different. We rely so much on other senses.'

I did wonder if his radio picture received way back in Sagittarius had shown him the rough scratchy boards from which the hut was built and the peeling paint and the large nail which he was about to step on. I suppose it might have done because he moved his foot neatly and avoided the nail. I wondered what sense he was using there.

'And what brought *you* here, Tony?' asked John Plowman with perhaps just a little hint of something in his voice.

'I just brought Dave in for a look round.' I didn't have to introduce them; they knew each other already.

'Oh yes.' His eyes flickered over the drawers. We hadn't left any scratches on the drawers, but one of the envelopes of herbs had dribbled on the floor. He knew what we had done.

'I hope you feel all right, Tony?' he said gently. 'That stuff is strong.'

'I feel *gorgeous*,' said Dave.

'I think he's had a little too much,' I said.

'No permanent harm,' said John. 'Just a simple little herbal remedy.' He smiled. 'It relaxes the nerves. It's a slight sudorific, too.'

100

'What's that mean?' said Dave.

'It means you sweat,' I told him.

'In fact, that's its main effect,' said John, giving us a sweet smile. 'It's not dangerous.'

'No,' I said. 'Unless it relaxes the nerves too far?'

'What does that mean?'

'I mean it could relax your nerves so far you didn't care what you did. Or didn't notice danger.'

'But I know its correct use. I would never misuse it.'

'I know you wouldn't, John. But I've been thinking about those missing children. And now Tom Butt. Suppose *they* got a dose of it.'

'I don't believe that could happen.'

'You can see for yourself anyone could get at it.'

Dave giggled. I supposed he was thinking how clever he'd been.

'What a life,' he said.

'No,' I said, watching John Plowman. 'I think we're getting on.'

'Murder's always serious,' John said, frowning. 'So, of course, I'm taking what you say seriously. But I don't think any of my herbal drops can have been used to harm any of the people you mention.' He always had a slightly cagey, legalistic way of phrasing things so that you wondered what he really had in reserve.

Dave gave another laugh.

'Don't let it get on your nerves,' I said aside to him.

'What murder?' said Mr Jasna, who had been showing signs of unease. I suppose they didn't have murder on Sagittarius.

'It's been in the papers,' I said. 'The children that disappear. I suppose they are dead. And then there's the young man, Tom Butt. I don't know if they've been taken out into space and left there, if they've all really been given another life on another planet, but what it all comes down to is what we on this earth call murder.'

John was pale, but so indeed was Mr Jasna. He looked at his watch, which was a good earth sort, the same as mine.

'I'll have to go,' he said in a practical voice. 'I have to get to work, it's my night turn.'

'Work?' I said, surprised.

'Naturally I have an earth-space-time identity too,' he explained in a kind voice. 'It's more convenient that way.'

'Yes,' I said. I could see it would be.

'You couldn't bear to see me as I really am.'

'No?'

We shook hands with him and my hot earth hand, which was indeed sweating profusely as John had prophesied, touched his cold paw.

'You feel cold,' I said, surprised.

'I cannot alter my basic temperature,' he said, rather sadly. 'I remain basically what I am, what I am.'

He saluted and walked out. It took me a moment to recover from that chill from Sagittarius.

'He's one of your best,' I said to John Plowman. 'That is he will be. I can see the quality. But he's not performing yet, is he?'

'He has some very interesting points,' said John Plowman in a detached way. 'You are cold and refuse to open your arms. Who can tell what you miss? One day, perhaps, a visitor will come for me, and off I will go with him.'

'He didn't like hearing about murder, did he? I suppose you can't blame him. But I've been thinking about things and this is what I think. There's too much coincidence about the dates those children disappeared and the dates we happened, or a group of us happened to be out on trips for the Club. I see that. Will the police see it? And if so, who will they suspect? A visitor from outer space or one of us? And if one of us, which one? You, me, Cyrus Read?'

'You mean Cyrus Read, of course,' said John smoothly.

'I'm not committing myself to what I mean. It's not as simple as that.' And really it wasn't. All this time Dave was staring at us with wide open eyes. More new ideas were coming to him than he'd had for a long time, and he was a boy who was tenacious of ideas.

'Well, I have a surprise for you,' said John. 'I've had a talk with the police. And I can add up and do mental arithmetic too. The policeman didn't say much. Men like him never do, but I just gave him what facts I had.'

'The same as I would do,' I said.

'Of course, and he was interested. I don't deny it. He *was* interested.'

'I think there may be some things I know and you don't, and that I might tell.'

'Of course. There always are. Be careful, though, won't you?'

'What do you mean?'

'I mean that he *is* the police. I personally have always found him very friendly. But I think one always runs a certain risk in coming forward.'

'But you came forward.'

'Did I say that? No, *they* came to me asking questions. I only told them what they wanted to know.'

I frowned. He was saying things I didn't want to hear. Sometimes the onlooker sees more of the game and so on, you know the saying. Perhaps he was the onlooker who had seen.

'Come on, Dave,' I said, 'we'll be pushing off.'

I won't come right out and say what he was hinting at,

tape, because I dare say it is guessable, but the feeling I had when I heard about the children, that long shudder, that entry into misery, looked like being thoroughly justified.

'Well, I suppose I'll be round later in the week,' I said to him.

'Yes.' He hesitated. 'Maybe no meeting this week. I have a lot on hand.'

'Mr Jasna?'

'He's worth thinking about,' he said cautiously. 'And then there's a man over at Ealing who says he can control machines with his mind. He's already made a start with his own electric razor. Says it attacked him one morning but now he's got it under control.'

I knew then that he wasn't a bit put out at the insurrection organized by Esther Glasgow, that he might even have helped it on, because he was getting ready to move on to a new interest. Always in the past, I'd been the one to walk out on a club. This time it was happening to me.

I took Dave home. I thought he seemed more or less all right. I wondered how much there was in that drug talk and how much John had been pulling my leg. Then I came home, avoiding my sister Jean, and started to pour myself out on to my tape.

I wasn't happy. John Plowman had more or less told me that if I went to the police they would look at me with speculative eyes. Without my knowing it, probably I was already a suspect. But then, we all were. All the same, I thought I'd go and see them. And then I thought after all I'd leave it.

I swung to and fro. I played the tape again to myself, wondering if any new noise would have crept on to it. But it was dead.

I went downstairs and sat in the kitchen. Jean was there.

'Have they come home yet?' I asked mechanically, but I could see on her face that there was no news yet of the missing two, Belle and her brother.

'Did you teach Belle?' I asked.

'I think I've taught all of them,' said Jean in a whisper. 'Anyway, I know them. So do you.'

'Only through you.' I wasn't looking at her, so I didn't see her face till she touched my arm. Then I saw she was crying.

'There was blood on your shirt, Tony,' she said. 'Maybe you didn't know, but I found it there.'

We sat in silence. Then I said, 'The blood doesn't mean anything. All that talk about blood is nonsense. I probably cut myself.'

'You'll go to the police, won't you?' she asked.

'Yes. I'll go.'

'I'll come with you.'

'No. I don't want you coming with me like a mother.'

And I heaved myself up out of my chair. Misery is a big, big city to walk into, but when you've got to its heart then you certainly know you are there.

I could hear the child next door still hooting and crying. He'd been at it all day.

I'd go to the police. If they all had minds like Jean it would be a risk, I thought, but a calculated risk. A risk I'd have to take. I owed it to Tom.

Chapter Ten

Inspector Dove had his car back and still hadn't discovered who had lost the child's rubber duck. He had put it aside, not thinking it would ever be claimed now.

'Someone's crying for that, I bet,' he said.

But he said it mechanically. It wasn't something he was really thinking about. Perhaps he had a slight passing thought in his mind about his car, which had disappeared and come back. There had been a rash of stolen cars in the district in the last few weeks. And the most popular type to steal seemed to be Fords. You can steal them in any colour, this thief seemed to be saying to himself, so long as it's a Ford.

They were walking on the edge of violence in Coffin's bailiwick these days. The disappearance of the two last children, Belle and her brother, had sharpened fears to the point where they were bound to cut someone soon.

Coffin was in his room with Dove when Tony Young asked to see him.

'I'm too busy,' he said to the constable who brought the message. 'Give him to someone else.'

'Parr thought there was something worth thinking about with this Young,' said Dove. 'It's in his notes.'

'All right, let Parr see him then.'

'Parr's out, sir,' said the constable. 'He had a message a minute ago and went out.'

'Let Young wait till he comes back then.'

Tony Young waited some time. When Parr eventually came to him, his plump face was unfriendly. He looked at Tony without speaking, then sat down. They were alone together in a small bare room which was used for such interviews. A former occupant, while waiting as Tony had waited, had chipped a large circle in the plaster of the wall, and no one had tried to do much about it. After all, they were moving soon, weren't they?

'Well?' said Parr.

'My sister, Jean,' began Tony nervously. He hadn't meant to be nervous, but he was. The wait had achieved what Coffin had probably meant it to achieve. 'Jean,' he said again. It was a bad beginning and he knew it.

Parr didn't answer, but the figure of Jean was behind his eyes. He waited for Tony to begin again.

'I just came round.' He hesitated again, then said, with a touch of the old Tony, 'Well, say *something*.'

'Go on.'

'Thanks. That's a help. Now I know how you feel.' His voice shook.

Parr was still slow to speak. Perhaps he wanted Tony to see that no, he didn't know how he felt.

'I came round here because I wanted to say something.'

'Go on,' said Parr again.

'If my sister ever goes out with you, she'll want her head examined,' said Tony vindictively.

'Let's leave that, shall we? Go on as if you've never spoken,' said Parr.

'About Tom Butt. And the children.'

Now Parr relented. He got out his cigarettes and offered one. 'Now take your time,' he said. 'Don't rush.'

'I don't smoke. And don't run up any flags. I know you policemen. I'm not confessing.'

'Who said anything about a confession?'

'You. You shouted it out loud without saying a word.

Let's make it easy for him, you said, he's come to tell all. Well, I came to help you.'

'Almost everyone says that,' said Parr.

'Jean says I'd better come. I always do what she says. And so will you in the end.'

'You better get on with what you've got to say.'

'I run a Club. You know that?'

'I know about it.'

'Yes, of course you do. I suppose you think we're all crazy, but we're not. We've got our reasons for what we do. Different reasons, some of us.' He stopped.

'Yes, go on. Different reasons?' Parr wasn't as yet a skilled interrogator; he was only learning. At the moment he hadn't developed a style of his own; he was imitating his boss.

'Well, different reasons. I won't go into those now. Anyway, you know what we do. As well as having meetings we get reports on UFO sightings and if it's within range off we go. John's got a motor bike and one of the girls, Esther Glasgow, can borrow her father's car. Another member, old Miss Jones, has an old car that works if we don't use it too often; it's old like her, see. We manage. Well, what I've noticed is that always when one of these children has disappeared, it coincided with the date of one of our little checking expeditions.'

'So?' prompted Parr.

'I know it could be just coincidence.'

'And why did you think it wasn't?'

'Well, in spite of what people say it's easier to believe in a *reason* than just plain chance. I suppose it's because we always want to believe in *intelligence*.'

'And whose intelligence were you believing in?'

'I had to ask myself if it was a human intelligence at all.' Tony looked warily at Parr. But Parr did not laugh.

108

Indeed, his features tightened somewhat. Cautiously, Tony went on. 'It didn't seem likely, though, that a vehicle from outer space had landed round here and taken off any of the children. There would have been *some* external evidence, I thought. Of course, I know what John Plowman says: that the operation of physical laws *can* appear to work miracles, that that is what a miracle is, the laws of the universe working in a way beyond our understanding. But I couldn't seem to accept a miracle.'

Parr said nothing, but looked as though miracles wasn't his word for it either.

'So then I had to ask myself if it was one of *us*, somehow using the opportunities of these expeditions. I wondered if perhaps these trips didn't provide some sort of conditions that made any abductions possible. Perhaps this character could only get out at such times, or something like that. I was looking round for an answer, you see.'

'Yes, I do see,' said Parr, a little grimly.

'I even thought that perhaps some sort of drug was involved. I still think there could be something like that.'

Parr nodded. He waited, but Tony had no more to say. 'And that's all?' said Parr.

'That's all.'

'You haven't got any names to offer?'

Tony shook his head silently.

'Right.' Parr got up. Tony got up, too. 'You're not going?' he said with some anxiety.

'I'll be back.'

'But you haven't said anything.'

'All right,' said Parr. 'Thank you. Will that do?'

He went out and left Tony alone. He met Dove in the corridor, who looked enquiringly. 'He says he doesn't believe in miracles and it was a human agency,' said Parr.

'That's what I believe, too,' said Dove sourly.

'Us and who else?' said Parr.

'The kid's not speaking,' said Dove. 'Not yet, anyway. He came back two hours ago, by the way, but his mother took her time letting us know.'

Parr left him and went into the room where his boss Coffin was standing by the window. He listened to what Parr had to tell him.

'Yes,' he said. 'Interesting. Not the way he thinks it is, of course. Brave of him, really, to put his head into the lion's den.'

'I would say he is quite frightened,' said Parr. 'More than he cares to admit.'

'Well, go back in to him and bring him along to see me.'

'All right,' said Parr and went along the corridor to the interrogation room which wasn't really very far away and spoke to Tony.

'The boss wants to have a word with you.'

'What about?' Tony was nervous.

'What about? What do you think? What you just told me.'

'Oh.' Tony considered. 'So that really was something then?'

Parr smiled. Not perhaps the very nicest smile in the world, nor were his motives good in smiling it. He wanted to alarm Tony and to dominate him at the same time. All this was reflected very accurately in the smile and Tony saw.

'I didn't think you'd take me seriously.'

'Yes, I can see that now.'

Tony studied Parr's face. 'Has something happened? Something I don't know about?'

Parr shrugged.

'You look as though something has happened.'

Parr took a risk. 'One of the children has been found.'

'Oh,' Tony went white. From his pocket he took out a big pair of tinted spectacles and put them on.

'You often wear those?' asked Parr with interest.

'No. Just sometimes.'

'They alter you a bit. Hide your face.'

'You think that's why I wear them?'

'I just noticed it,' said Parr. 'After all, you put them on.'

'I think you're deliberately working on me. Trying to make me nervous. I don't think you *have* found a girl.'

'Did I say found?'

'I thought you did.'

'Well, it was a mistake. Perhaps I should say "came back".'

'How did she come back? Did she walk back? How was she?'

Parr said: 'No one told me.'

'Was there – was there any blood on her?'

'Did you think there might be?'

'I shouldn't have asked,' said Tony, tormented.

'It doesn't matter,' said Parr politely.

'It always matters when you speak out of turn.'

'I meant it doesn't matter what questions you ask me because I have to take you in to see my boss now.' He was still being polite. He led the way to the door.

'I bet he didn't tell you to tell me about the girl coming back,' said Tony suddenly. He took off his spectacles, revealing his bright blue eyes. 'I bet you took a risk. And now you're regretting it.'

Coffin was waiting for them in his room. He had moved away from the window and was sitting at his desk. He and Tony knew each other by sight and Tony knew that his girl friend Judith was a friend of Coffin's wife. But it didn't seem the time to acknowledge any relationship and they both looked at each other silently, summing up.

'I'm sorry I had to keep you waiting.'

'I thought you did it on purpose.' Tony had recovered his nerve and was getting more aggressive.

'In a way. It wasn't an accident, anyway.'

'I thought not.'

'I mean that something happened.' He's clever, thought Coffin.

He's cleverer than I thought, said Tony inwardly. He hardly ever thought anyone over the age of twenty-five was clever, having an unconscious belief that mental deterioration set in around then. In most of the people around him it was true, of course.

'It was good of you to come in, Mr Young. We do get quite a lot of people coming in with stories. It's one of the reasons I had to keep you waiting now.'

'Oh, good.'

Coffin looked enquiring.

'I mean I thought *I* might be the reason you had to keep me waiting,' said Tony. 'I sort of got the idea from Sergeant here that you were interested in me.'

'We're interested in all young men in your age group who live in this district and fly kites of any sort.'

'Do I fly a kite?'

'Higher and higher,' said Coffin.

'Yes, well, I suppose I asked for that. But I didn't like the sergeant coming round and asking for my fingerprints.'

'We're asking for every man's. Everyone who can count as a man.'

'You can have mine now, if you like.'

'Later.'

'It's late now.'

112

It was still day enough to see the street through the window, and from where Tony sat with the light full in his face, he could see the new police station across the way. Construction hadn't stopped on it, in spite of missing Tom Butt, and the building was beginning to look more like a building ever day. It was going to be very ugly.

'You know, you could be in serious trouble,' said Coffin. 'You refuse a fingerprint, you come in here offering information, which doesn't amount to much if I may say so, and you have other liabilities too.'

'Such as?'

'Well, that'll come out as you go along.'

Coffin's voice was neither kind nor unkind, simply as if he knew all the rules and could see the picture and where Tony fitted into it. Tony began to understand where he had put himself.

'Not if I stop talking.'

'You won't stop talking, Tony. Not now. You can't.'

And it was true. You can reach a point when the words themselves have taken over and one leads on to another. That is the danger of tape recorders.

'Anyway, it's as well you came. Let's have everything out.'

Out, like a box of bricks, child's toys, Tony thought.

'There's only what I've told you,' said Tony. 'And what you haven't told me.'

'Let's go on then from what you've told us.'

'I've said it once. I don't want to waste time and energy going over it again.'

'But you've got lots of time and energy to spare. That's one of the things I've noticed about you. You run risks when you've got as much extra as you have.'

Tony looked at him warily.

113

'Now you came round here with a story, with information. But there's something more than that, isn't there?'

'I don't know why you say that,' said Tony after a pause.

'Because in my experience there nearly always is. What is it? Where's it coming from? Is it your sister? Some trouble about her?'

Parr shifted uneasily. This was an area he didn't like.

'*No*,' said Tony.

'She knows all the missing children though.'

'Leave Jean alone.'

'Sisters often cover up for their brothers. Especially if they stand in the relationship of a mother to them.'

'Jean's no mother to me.'

'No.' Coffin studied Tony's face. 'But something is worrying you. You feel guilty about something. You look it, too. Is it the two children, the brother and sister? Is there something about their disappearance?'

'That doesn't worry me. I don't feel guilty about them.'

'There's only one thing left. Tom Butt. It's Tom Butt that's upsetting you.'

'I don't feel guilty,' muttered Tony.

'But responsible.'

'I might be. I just might be.'

There was a long pause. Coffin knew he had got somewhere, that things were moving at last.

'Get the boy a cup of coffee,' he said to Parr, 'and ring up his sister and tell her we've got him here and that he's all right. She might be worrried.'

When the coffee came, they both drank it thirstily.

'I knew Tom a bit. A bit more than I've said.'

'Yes. You were at school together. Some other boy's fingerprints in Tom's room. Would they match with yours?'

'He could have had other friends,' said Tony. 'First

thing I want to say is that Tom was not a jokey boy at all. He was dead serious. And the other thing I want to say is that I'm not a jokey boy either. So what we did had a meaning. In a way.' He paused.

'Go on.'

'When he was a kid Tom thought he could fly. There's nothing in that, lots of kids have fantasies and they forget them when they're older, but Tom didn't forget his. I think he half believed he *had* been able to fly. The way he'd dreamt it, he'd flown off and disappeared. Or the flying act and the disappearing were the same thing. It wasn't clear.'

'But *you* didn't believe it.'

Tony shrugged. 'I believe what I see. I haven't seen anything positive yet.'

'Someone did believe it, though.'

'Yes. John Plowman did. He heard about it and asked to see Tom. I said to Tom – let's *make* you seem to fly. He didn't like the idea at first, but he wanted to be friends.'

'And what were you going to do?'

Tony paused. 'I'd really been looking for someone like Tom for some time.' He paused again, as if waiting for them to speak, which they did not. 'I told you I had a serious purpose. I'll explain.' He was getting into his stride. 'John knew about Tom, was interested, perhaps half believed in him already. That was my beginning.'

'And what was your end?'

'A test. I thought I'd make Tom a test case. Let's see what old John makes of him, I thought. Let Tom disappear. *I* know it's a fake. I wanted to see what John did.'

Coffin raised his eyebrows.

'I wanted to see if John Plowman went for fakes,' said Tony bluntly.

'So all the apparatus of Tom Butt's disappearance was a fake?'

'I thought it was. It was meant to be. I arranged it all – voice on the telephone – it was Tom himself, of course. You can speak on that telephone from more than one point. We left the clothes in the lift, to create an illusion Tom had been there. That *was* the plan.' Unconsciously, he put an accent on the verbs.

'And when did it go wrong?'

'From the beginning, really. Tom got frightened. "Maybe I *will* disappear", he said. He had this thought, you see, that he *had* once disappeared. He had a lot of superstitions. He thought he could tell the future. He couldn't tell his own, though.'

'Perhaps he could,' said Coffin grimly. 'So what's your theory? Someone stepped in and made your plan real?'

'I think Tom told someone.'

'And that someone killed him? Why?'

'There must be a reason.'

'But you don't know it?'

'You don't believe me,' said Tony. 'You think it was me.'

'You seem very closely involved in it all.'

'Yes, I know,' said Tony bitterly. 'Too close. I'd better tell you this. I've got a tape-recorder. You've got one yourself.' He glanced across the room. 'Did you ever go to it one day and find there were sounds, voices on it that you hadn't put there?'

'No.'

'No. It wouldn't happen to you. But it did to me. I thought it was a child calling and crying. Just snatches, you know. Jumbled up and indistinct as if taken from some way away.'

'You'd better give me this tape,' said Coffin.

116

'The sounds were there one day, then gone the next,' said Tony. He looked pink cheeked and young and nervous. 'Maybe I imagined them. That's the best thing to think, isn't it.'

'For you it probably is,' said Coffin. 'But unless you suffer from hallucinations, it's probably not true. Do you suffer from hallucinations?'

Tony pulled a face.

'You could have put them there yourself. And erased them.'

'I didn't do that.'

'Or you could be telling lies all round the clock,' went on Coffin, ignoring him. 'But anyway, suppose you let me have the tape?'

'Yes. You can have it. You'll have to let me go and get it, though.'

'No. You stay here.' He gave Parr a look. 'We'll go.'

'Jean won't like that. Why not me?'

Coffin did not answer.

Usually when you ask a child a question he will give you the answer he thinks you want to have. Belle's brother was doing his best.

He had come wandering in, grubby and thirsty, about two hours ago. Alone and without Belle.

'Where's Belle?'

He shook his head.

'Where have you been? Where have you been hiding?'

In slightly varying forms these were the two questions that first his parents, then the police asked. Where's your sister and where have you been?

To the first he shook his head, and to the second he said: 'in a little house.' He repeated it hoarsely: 'in a little house.' It seemed a good answer to him, but he was only three years old.

His mother began to cry.

'What have you come back for?' said Jean, as she opened the front door to Parr.

'Your brother sent me to get his tape recorder.'

'Tony sent you? That doesn't sound like him. Still, you'd better have it.' She led him upstairs and watched nervously as he went into the room. Tony had left it tidy. She pointed. 'There it is – on the table.'

'Thanks.'

Silently they went downstairs together.

'Goodnight and thanks again,' said Parr.

She held the door open. 'Are you keeping Tony?'

'Of course not.'

'Will he be home tonight?'

'I expect so. Don't worry, Jean.' The name slipped out and he coloured. He had red hair and the thin skin that goes with it.

'Well, I do worry. I worry over Tony. You have to.'

When he got back, Parr handed the tape and the machine over to Tony who considered for a moment and then handed it over to Coffin.

'Here,' he said.

'You look as though you're thinking thoughts,' said Coffin.

'Yes,' said Tony, 'thinking thoughts.'

Afterwards when Tony had to describe the moment to himself, he said: So I gave up the tape and stepped out as a commentator. From now on I was an actor, and as liable to get mauled as anyone else.

118

Chapter Eleven

In the small hours Tony Young was sent home. His sister Jean called to him from her bedroom, where she was lying awake, when she heard him on the stairs. 'Tony? Oh, I'm so glad you're back.' He stood at her bedroom door and looked at her. 'Of course I'm back.' She looked at her clock. 'After midnight. What have you been doing?' Tony sighed. 'I've been doing what's known as "helping the police with their enquiries". If I ever read that in the papers I shall know exactly what it means. How many hours hanging around, how much waiting while someone does something mysterious down the corridor that they're never quite specific about. How many cups of tea you get offered. How much . . . '

Jean spoke sharply from her pillows. 'Shut up, Tony, and go to bed. You're all wound up.'

Tony went to bed, in his room which seemed strangely empty without the tape recorder he had come to regard as his other self; he did not sleep much.

No one who knew the Anderson boy was back without his sister, slept much that night.

Coffin didn't try to go to bed at all. He played Tony's tape. He listened to his own and dictated a few notes for it. Then he lay down on the camp bed he had had made up in one corner of his office and waited for the nearly summer dawn to come creeping into the room.

He had the feeling that, although he could do nothing while it was dark, he wanted to be on the alert. But in spite of himself his eyes closed. He had omitted to telephone his wife. In the morning he might, or he might not be greeted with anger. She was a little undisciplined in her moods at the moment. He never knew whether he was going to be greeted with chilling nonchalance or real enthusiasm. Some of it was his fault, he wasn't sure how much.

He came awake to hear the telephone ringing and as he had expected it was his wife.

'Where are you?' she said.

'You know already.' Why answer a rhetorical question, she knew where he was all right or why was she ringing? But you couldn't say anything.

'It's morning now.'

'Yes, I can see it.' He squinted at the sky. Raining. But daylight was struggling through.

'There *was* a night in between.'

He paused. The trouble with the telephone line, as with a tape recorder, was that it didn't register the quality of your silence. This silence of his was apologetic, defensive and hopeful. He was hopeful that his wife would yet pack up the quarrel and put it away.

But surprisingly, it got across. He heard her sigh. 'I wish I didn't worry over you. But I do worry.'

'I'm really all right and I *should* have let you know.'

'I'm just making the coffee. Will you be home for breakfast?'

'Don't wait. I'll try in about an hour.'

Satisfied and apparently cheerful, she rang off. It was the day's little miracle. No others followed.

The news that Belle's brother had returned, but not Belle, had become public. There was a small crowd hanging about outside the police station and a slightly larger one outside Belle's home.

There was a strange atmosphere everywhere.

'Don't you feel the violence there crackling under your feet as you walk the pavements?' said Coffin to Dove, who had just come in.

'I didn't walk,' said Dove, who had a literal mind.

'Oh, yes.' Coffin turned away from the window. 'Your car all right? Find out who'd lost the rubber duck?'

'I've had other things to do.' He dumped a file of reports and statements on the table in front of his chief. 'There's nothing there, but you'll want to read them,' he said with a virtuous air.

'Yes, well I have different ideas,' said Coffin, pushing them aside. 'Get me one of the girls.' They had three women attached to the station as aides. Their duties were usually concerned with women and children. They didn't lead quiet lives.

'They're already worked off their feet,' said Dove.

'I only want one.'

'When they first came you wouldn't use them at all, now you're working them all the time,' said Dove.

'They don't argue back like some of my colleagues.'

Coffin had no favourite among the three policewomen and didn't seem to distinguish between them. And they, finding him rather alarming, didn't try to get closer. 'I don't think he knows one of us from the other,' said Joan Eames. But he did. He knew that Joan Eames was the one who was always a bit late and came hurrying in for duty, not quite making it at a run, but moving fast. He knew that Lucy Bates had an allergy of some sort which resulted in bursts of sneezing periodically. He had heard it was caused by wood dust, in which case she was in for a thin time when they moved to the new building. Thirdly, he knew that Katerina McKenzie, who had a German mother and Scottish father, moved silently and neatly and that if the door closed quietly and someone

121

slid into the room then it was Katerina who had arrived. Joan banged doors.

This time the door banged and someone hurried in, so he knew it was Joan he had got.

'Good morning,' he said politely. He had already learnt it paid to be polite to Joan; it gave her time to get her breath back.

'What have you got lined up for this morning?' he asked.

Joan took a deep breath and started: 'Nine-thirty, magistrates' court, two boys shop-lifting. Ten-thirty, visit to child welfare officer about a child-cruelty case. Eleven, interview with Vicar of St Mary's, but I'll be late for *that*, and before I start out I've got my notes to do and . . .'

'Then you have between now and nine-thirty to do something for me,' said Coffin, looking at the clock.

'Oh yes?'

'I want you to take a child for a walk.'

'Just me?'

'Well, you'd better take his mother too. To tell you the truth, I don't suppose she'd let him out of her sight just now.'

'We won't have a crowd following us, will we?'

'I'll fix that,' said Coffin, looking out of the window. 'I don't suppose you'll have to walk far. He's only small and the doctor who examined him last night says there's no sign he's been walking around a lot. Feet weren't bruised or sore or anything like that . . . I'll give you the medical report, you'd better read it before you meet him.' He tossed it over and Joan caught it. 'You were a nurse before you came into the Force, weren't you?' She nodded. 'It'll mean more to you, then. Also it might help with the boy. Watch him all you can. See what you make of him. Watch the mother, too.'

'What?'

'Watch the mother,' said Coffin, not amplifying the statement.

'You think she's important?'

'I think she may be everything,' he said.

'Will you be there?'

'No.' He got up, ending the interview. 'Not exactly there, but around.'

'What do you think he meant about the mother?' Joan Eames said to Sergeant Parr downstairs as she gathered up her things. She occasionally found it possible to strike up a human relationship with him, which was not the way she felt about Inspector Dove.

'Oh, I dunno. He's a bit of an old joss at the moment. I suppose mothers are always important.'

'Was your mother important?'

'Rather. Still is. She's looking out for a good girl for me to marry.' He grinned at her.

Joan nodded. She liked him; she had a strong idea she could like him rather a lot, but she had no idea how he felt about her. As Tony Young might have put it, his signals to her were contradictory.

'Well, I'm going out to see this boy and his mother and together we're going to see if he will take us to the place where he hid.'

'Looks a good idea,' said Parr. 'He ought to know.'

'You're not too well acquainted with children, are you?' said Joan, preparing to depart. 'You're an only child, I should think?'

'Yes, I am. How did you know?'

Joan laughed. 'Perhaps it's the way you talk about your mother,' she said over her shoulder. 'Anyway, I'll tell you. The boy ought to know, but will he *say*?'

Mrs Anderson had been told to expect Joan Eames and

was waiting for her. The front door swung open as soon as Joan appeared.

The two women stared at each other. 'I thought you'd be older,' said Mrs Anderson.

'I'm older than I look. Can I come in?'

For answer, Mrs Anderson held the door open wider and stood aside, but she didn't say anything.

Joan looked at her with sympathy. 'You look tired,' she said.

'I'm afraid the house is very untidy,' said the woman defensively. 'I haven't been able to give my mind to it.'

'I should think not.'

In fact the hall where they stood was not untidy, but it was undusted and the flowers on the small round table where the telephone stood were dead. They had been dead for days.

'Is the boy ready?' asked Joan.

'Yes, I'll get him.' She left Joan standing in the hall and went into a room at the end of it.

Joan looked around while she waited. Before disaster struck the household it had been a neat and well-decorated hall, the home of people who enjoyed living there. The furnishings were not expensive (you didn't live in this district if you could afford to move) but they were carefully chosen. On the other hand, the taste it displayed was commonplace and unimaginative. It could have been duplicated twenty times up and down Saxe-Coburg Street. The only exceptional thing was the telephone; working-class households in Saxe-Coburg Street didn't have telephones.

Mrs Anderson came back, holding her son by the hand. 'We have to have the telephone,' she said, seeing Joan's gaze. 'It's my husband's work. At the docks. They have to be able to let him know.' She didn't specify what, possibly she did not know. Men around here were not talkative about their work at home.

'Oh yes.' Joan was looking at the boy. He was wearing a tweed coat, a cap and thick socks up to his knees. 'Isn't he a little wrapped up for such a warm day?'

'He's a delicate boy; he needs to be wrapped up; he's had a shock.'

'I thought the doctor said he was all right.'

'He's still had a shock. Haven't you, baby boy?' Baby boy gave his mother a blank, possibly hostile stare. Her hands shook as she adjusted his coat.

If he hasn't had a shock, you have, thought Joan Eames. 'Ready?'

'Yes, come along, Baby.'

Baby was three and could walk and talk, but he wasn't doing either. His mother had picked him up in her arms.

'I should let him walk,' said Joan.

'Oh no, no. He'd be frightened.'

'He *has* to walk. He can't show us where to go unless he walks. Talk to him. Ask him to show us where he was hiding.'

'I've asked him that and he doesn't answer.'

'Yes, but he might be able to show us. Ask him to lead the way. Go on, put him down and ask him to do that.'

Mrs Anderson seemed to take a decision. She set the boy down. 'Come on, darling,' she said. 'Show us where Belle is.'

Something in her voice got across to Joan Eames. She doesn't mind so much about Belle, she thought. She's got back the one she likes best.

For a moment Joan was angry, then she looked at the woman's face and realized that any partiality Mrs Anderson felt was so deep rooted, so built into her character that she herself was unconscious of it. She was just a woman who thought boys were best.

'Bring him along,' said Joan gently.

Together they stepped out into the street. It was still early in the day and the street was not crowded. Far from it, in fact it was so empty of life that Joan suspected the hand of her boss, John Coffin, of having cleared it. At the end of the road there was a car and she thought she could see him sitting in it. So they were to be watched on their walk. She felt a little easier. Of course, it couldn't be dangerous, this walk of theirs, but it was nice to know someone was there.

'Show us where you came from,' said Joan to the boy. 'Show us the way. A clever boy like you can do that.'

He looked at her, as if amused, but did not move.

'Oh, come on, the way to Belle. Sister Belle?'

'She's not his sister,' said the woman suddenly, harshly. 'Not a full sister, that is. You shouldn't say she is.'

'I thought she was.'

'She's not my husband's child. She was born before I married him. He took her on. He's been very good.'

So that's why you don't like her, thought Joan. 'Should you say it in front of him?' she said, nodding towards the boy. 'He may not like it.'

'Sister,' said the boy speaking for the first time in a rough little voice, as if he hadn't used it for a long time. 'Sister,' he said again.

'Well, that's what he thinks,' said Joan. 'Show us the way then, love.'

He started forward confidently and the two women followed. Their little party, followed at a discreet distance by the police car, went down the road, turned a corner and headed towards the river. Ahead of them was a long street with the school on one side and the trees of a small park on the other. Joan thought maybe he was leading them towards the school. Their pace quickened.

'He's taking us to the park, you know,' said his mother. 'He always likes to go to the park.'

'Perhaps his sister is there. Perhaps that's where he hid, it's reasonable.'

'It was all searched,' said Mrs Anderson. Mutely Joan admitted the improbability of any hiding place in the park being overlooked.

They stood at the park gate and looked at the neat paths, the flower-beds and the trim green grass lawns. There was a pool in one corner and at the opposite one the children's playground.

'Swings?' said the boy hopefully, stepping out briskly towards the playground.

'No, no swings,' said Joan Eames severely. 'Belle! Belle! Show us where you were hiding when you stayed away from Mummy.'

'Ask him about the little house,' said his mother. 'That's what he said: that he was in a little house.'

'All right,' said Joan. 'Show us the little house. Where is it?'

Slowly their party set off again. This time, after hesitating at the gate, they walked back the way they had come. Very soon they had reached the main road and were heading down Saxe-Coburg Street.

This time, except for traffic, nothing very positive stretched ahead of them. It seemed as though they might walk on for ever.

'Is he likely to have walked far from home?' asked Joan. 'Can he walk much distance?'

'He's strong for his age. I should think he could walk quite a long way if he had to.'

'He'd have been noticed, wouldn't he, if he'd come far on his own?'

'I think so. But you can't be sure,' said his mother. Then she said: 'He likes walking.'

'I'm beginning to notice that.' He liked the traffic too, and Joan thought he was really strolling along, enjoying it without much more in his head. 'He can't have come this way,' she said. They stopped. Gently she said again to the child: 'Take us to the little house where you were with Belle. Please do that.'

He was silent, evidently considering, and then he took Joan Eames's hand and started off.

'He doesn't talk much, does he?'

'He does sometimes. When he wants to.'

They turned off the main road again down a side street. Behind them as before came the attendant police car. She was very conscious of this following and she wondered if the Andersons were too. Mrs Anderson must have been because she continually looked back over her shoulder. As for the boy, he, although silent, gave every sign of being so sharp and bright that Joan quite expected him to stop and ask for a lift.

The geography of this district was simple. There were two wide roads, Upper Dock Road and Saxe-Coburg Street, down which traffic poured and these were bisected at intervals by lesser side roads, mainly residential but with the occasional factory and office block. None of it was new and none of it much pleasure to the eye. It was like a grid. Or a child's game. All you had to do was to keep walking round and round the squares and you got 'home'.

Mrs Anderson saw this before Joan did. 'Know what?' she said. 'He's taking us back home.'

'Oh blast.' Joan Eames knelt down and got her face on

a level with the small flushed one. (In spite of what his mother said, he was too well wrapped up.)

'The place where you hid?' she said hopefully. 'Take us there.'

'This isn't really a good place to stop,' fussed Mrs Anderson. Joan thought how she hated anyone coming between her and her son, even to ask a question.

'I want to see if he understands me.'

The police car also drew up and stopped. Coffin got out. 'No good?' he asked sympathetically. 'Doesn't he understand?'

'Of course he understands,' said his mother.

'Why doesn't he do something about it then?'

The women were silent, for once united. Their eyes met. Speechlessly they agreed that Coffin didn't know what he was talking about.

'He is trying,' said Joan Eames. 'Anyone can see he's trying.' She took his hand.

'It was a bad idea,' said Coffin gloomily. 'And yet, there it is, he knows, he's the only one who does. He ought to be able to tell us.'

With a radiant smile, the boy came up to him and touched his hand.

'You see, he *is* trying,' said Joan. They were halfway down Riga Street. Behind them was the blank wall of an old factory and in front were houses and a couple of shops. The factory, which looked empty and disused, had once made shoe polish. But its trade had dwindled and died as people seemed to give up cleaning their shoes. Or anyway they gave up cleaning them with Liddell's Boot and Shoe Polish. This factory had its front on Riga Street and its back on Archangel Street. (There was a strong Russian element in the street names here because the old Muscovite traders had lodged round here centuries ago.) A short cobbled way led into the factory through the high arched entrance under which huge horse-drawn drays had once come and gone.

The little party crossed this cobbled path. Joan looked up at the factory. 'What about there?' she said.

'We searched there,' said Coffin briefly. 'Of course.'

He got back into his car and watched them.

The boy was tugging at Joan Eames's hand. 'I think we're getting somewhere,' she called back.

'I'm coming,' she said to the boy. 'Don't pull too hard. Little house?'

'Little house. Little house.'

'We looked all round here,' said his mother. 'Everyone searched.' She was beginning to look white and haggard. Joan noticed she was beginning to put everything connected with Belle into the past tense.

'I think we have to try this,' said Joan. She was looking around her. They were passing a terrace of small houses, built of yellowing brick which soot and fog had darkened. Was one of these 'the little house'? It didn't seem likely, somehow. They were certainly small enough, but no smaller than the boy's own home and therefore probably just seemed normal, what a home should be, to him. And anyway, he was small himself and houses looked bigger then, didn't they? No, something in the phrase 'little house' suggested something special, something childlike.

Now they had passed houses and were coming up to two or three shops. She knew them and sometimes bought groceries here on her way home from work. She could see the grocery shop and the chemist shop next door, with its window full of aspirin and lipstick. Joan often wished the chemist shop was something like an American drug store and that you could get something to drink there. She could drink some coffee this minute. The third shop was a general store that sold everything the chemist and the grocer had forgotten to stock and one or two things they wouldn't have touched at any price. One window was full of magazines and comics, including a row of paperbacks which were hardly kids' stuff. It was a double-fronted shop and the farther window seemed to interest the child. He led the two women right up to it.

Joan Eames looked at it blankly, seeing a jumble of cheap toys.

'Lots of toys there,' she said.

'Little house,' he said, confidently pointing. 'Little house.' He gave her that same brilliant smile he had given to Coffin and which she already saw as having some special meaning.

She looked at rows of plastic money-boxes shaped into miniature houses with chimneys and window-boxes and a slot in the roof to put the money in.

'Yes, a little house. Lots of little houses,' she said sadly. She patted his head. 'Clever boy.'

She turned to his mother. 'Better get him home. This is over, I think.'

Silently they started to walk off. Joan Eames still had the boy's hand and she felt him dragging.

'Wait a minute,' she said. 'Let's go back, into the shop.' They went back.

'Well, he did try,' she said to his mother. 'I'd like to buy him a little house.'

'I'd rather have a horse,' said the boy very clearly and suddenly.

Joan looked down, surprised. 'So you *can* talk.'

'When he wants,' put in his mother.

If you didn't talk *for* him, he might talk more, thought Joan Eames.

131

Watch the mother, John Coffin had said to her. Well, she had watched the mother. As a result of watching the mother she had come to certain conclusions. There were two. Firstly that the mother did not much love her daughter who was missing; secondly that she too much loved her son. She thought the son knew this, and she suspected that the sister had known too.

'Hello, Mr Plowman,' she said to the man behind the counter. 'Not busy today?'

'Not so busy,' he said. Joan couldn't tell if he was pleased or displeased by the peace of his shop; you could never read his expression easily behind his big thick spectacles.

'Seen any flying saucers lately?'

'No.' He was polite, level voiced.

'I want a toy for this young boy.'

'Oh yes, I know him.'

Jim was staring up at him. No expression much there either.

'He wants a toy horse.'

'A little horse,' said Jim, in an adult manner.

'Oh yes, I have some round the back. Tony,' he called, 'bring out that box of little wooden horses that came in yesterday.'

'Right.' Tony Young came in through the door at the back of the shop, staggering slightly because the box was awkwardly big and he was only a small slight boy.

'Hello,' he said, looking at them through his dark spectacles, which rendered him, like his employer, expressionless and calm. The two faces, Tony's and Plowman's, seemed for a moment to mirror each other.

Chapter Twelve

'Do you know Tony Young?' asked Mrs Anderson in surprise.

'Oh yes.' Joan Eames didn't find it necessary to say that a neat little biography of Tony had been fed her by Inspector Dove and that she had had him pointed out to her as he left the police station. 'We haven't been introduced, but I know him. Does he always work in that shop?'

'On and off. Lately anyway. He's always around.'

'I've met Mr Plowman.' Once again, Joan did not find it necessary to explain that they had met professionally. They had suspected John Plowman of peddling pornography among his paperbacks and Joan had been part of the team that had gone around investigating. Her part had been small, just to walk in and out of the shop on two occasions and buy some books. Perhaps it had just been a dirty story about John Plowman, because nothing was ever found as far as Joan Eames knew. She would have been the first to admit however that she didn't know everything and that there might be more tucked away in the file about John Plowman than she knew. She knew there was a file.

Joan Eames saw Mrs Anderson and Jim to their house. At the door, she hesitated.

'Come in and have a cup of tea. Yes, do.'

'All right. Thanks. I'd be glad to.' She didn't really want the tea but she was remembering Coffin's advice – watch the mother.

'Come into the kitchen. It's very untidy, I'm afraid.'
Mrs Anderson put on the kettle and sat her son on a chair
by the table, where he started to play with his little
wooden horse. Joan thought he seemed quite contented,
as if he'd done his job for the day.

He began to bang his horse on the table and sing
loudly.

His mother hurried to him. 'No, be quiet. We mustn't
wake Daddy.'

'Oh, your husband's in?' said Joan, sitting down herself.

'Yes, he's lying down upstairs. He's been up all night
trying to help find Belle. He just walks the streets and
sometimes he calls her name out.'

He's more upset than you are, thought Joan, but she
didn't say so. But presently he came down the stairs and
into the kitchen, a thin, tall man with fair hair, already
going prematurely bald.

He stopped when he saw Joan Eames.

'This is the police lady,' said his wife.

'Yes, I know. I guessed.' He looked heavy-eyed and
exhausted. 'You didn't find anything?'

No one answered.

'No, I knew you wouldn't. How could you?'

'Someone will find something,' said Joan doggedly.

'Yes, but when will that be? And it'll be too late.'

This was indisputable and Joan didn't try to dispute it.
She glanced apprehensively at his wife, but she had her
eyes fixed on the kettle on the stove, as if she didn't want
to hear what was said.

'I can't help thinking that,' he said. 'All the time. You're
not doing enough.'

'We're doing a lot.' Joan Eames knew what they were
doing; knew how many men were working on it, asking
what questions and patiently hearing what answers.

'Not enough. Nothing's enough that doesn't work.'

'No.' This too was something Joan couldn't argue with. Who wanted to. You did your best, but it frequently wasn't enough. Joan Eames knew the statistics for unsolved crimes, this was part of the dark number of crimes that you didn't think about too much. Because if you did think about it too much, you might give up altogether, and go and do something quite different, like being a nurse.

'I suppose they've asked you this, but has Belle ever gone off on her own before?'

Husband and wife glanced at each other. 'Only playing,' said Mrs Anderson. 'She was playing in the garden and pretended to disappear. I grumbled at her for that.'

'Grumbled,' said her husband. 'You beat her.'

Mrs Anderson flushed. 'Well, it was a naughty thing to do.'

'You beat her *afterwards*. When you'd gone cold on it.'

'I wanted her to learn. It was wrong.'

'She was only playing.'

'Did she play on her own a lot? Or does she have friends?' put in Joan Eames.

'She has friends,' said Mr Anderson, breaking off his silent quarrel with his wife to look at Joan. 'All the girls in her class are her friends; all the girls in the streets round here are her friends. You ask and you'll see.' What he meant was: and only her mother wasn't her friend.

Joan drank her tea, said goodbye, and left the quiet bitter family behind her. She hadn't done much good with the boy, not what you could call a really good morning's work, but she hadn't entirely wasted her time.

Watch the mother, Coffin had advised, and she had watched the mother. She knew now that in this little family the mother was the one who wasn't happy. She wasn't happy, and presumably if she wasn't happy then the child Belle, who was missing, hadn't been happy either.

She went back to Coffin and reported this fact. It wasn't much, but it was what she had discovered.

She thought he didn't seem too surprised, as if it might have been what he was expecting to hear.

She had another thought too, but this she didn't pass on; it was that the boy looked cheerful and pleased with himself, and had accepted his present like a reward, as if he had somehow done what was expected of him.

Joan Eames reported back to Coffin, not to Inspector Dove, as she normally would have done, because this seemed expected of her. She was no nearer to feeling easy in John Coffin's presence, he was unnerving not friendly these days, but she felt that he had the case under control. It was an untidy case with far too many loose ends, but if anyone had them in a grasp, he had.

'I'm worried,' she said at once. 'I didn't do any good on this trip. And I saw things I'd rather not have seen.'

'That's what I sent you out for.'

'If you unturn a stone in family life then out crawls a slug. A group of little slugs maybe, none ready to kill but all ready to make you sick.'

'Perhaps it's not that bad,' said Coffin, after a pause. He may have been thinking about his own home life which, now she came to think of it, Joan Eames remembered was said to be not all that cosy. 'Don't go getting emotional.' He smiled. 'Or, as you wouldn't be much use deprived of *all* emotion, don't get *too* emotional. So all wasn't love and jam with the Andersons?'

'It was sort of cold and strange. I don't like to think what they're like when they're on they're own.'

'House tidy?'

'Not very. Was once.'

'You don't think the children were happy?'

'I don't know about the boy. I couldn't read him. And I've never seen the girl, but no, I don't think she was happy. I don't think she could have been. I wouldn't have been.' She poured out her impressions of the scene: mother, father, baby brother, friends, she described them all. She felt she was talking too much.

Coffin nodded. 'Now you can go out and see all the other mothers.'

'All the mothers?' She was appalled.

'Yes, the mothers and fathers and families of all the children who have disappeared. Go on around, talk to them, stay with them, live with them if they'll let you and then come back and tell me what sort of families they are.'

'And is this going to help?'

'I think it could help a lot.'

You didn't usually question your boss, but there was one question Joan Eames had to ask.

'I've read what's on the files about Tony Young. His statement about his alleged activities.' (Sometimes she just couldn't help talking that way.) 'Was he telling the truth?'

'Not all of it, no.'

'That's what I thought. I'd like to investigate him.'

'You may get a chance at that. But the families first, please.'

'I don't know if I'd be any good at it,' her voice faltered.

'You did a pretty good job on bringing back what I wanted from the Anderson family,' said Coffin; he was businesslike.

She got up to go. 'Right then. I'll do my best. And I'll

write up my notes on this and let you have it. That'll be it, I suppose?'

'Yes, you do that. But don't worry too much. I have it all here.' He patted a small machine by his side which had been faintly sighing and whirring all the time. 'I have it on a tape. I think I'll get more from hearing what you have to say than from anything you write. So whenever you've got something to say, drop in and have a talk.'

As she went out of the room, she thought that there were plenty of other tasks she could have been employed on and that this one looked as though it might take weeks. As if he was reading her thoughts, Coffin spoke:

'And in case you think you've got all the time in the world for it, let me tell you I can spare you exactly thirty-six hours.'

'Counting night and day?'

'Working round the clock,' he said with a laugh.

But it was a laugh that turned out serious. Even although she had the list of the families and where they lived already to hand, seeing them was an exhausting and time consuming task. There was also an element about it that she didn't quite like, of herself as predator. She felt she was hunting these people down.

As well as this, the task is repetitive. Seen close to, these families were all so different, withdraw a few feet and they were all so alike.

All of the families lived pretty close together in Archangel Street and Riga Street and Saxe-Coburg Street, so she took them in no special order but just as she found them in the house. On a couple of the houses she had to call twice. She was on her way to one of them, the Boyle household, now.

The Boyle household had lived with its tragedy for over

138

a year because Shirley Boyle had been the first child to go. Between her and the next child off there had been a gap of a year. This was something to think about, and the detectives had thought about it, but they hadn't really found themselves any proper answer. You could speculate that the murderer (only no one knew for sure yet if this person was a murderer) had been ill, absent or imprisoned.

She was apologetic at breaking in on the Boyle family at their meal and they were apologetic back to her because they were sitting there eating it.

She loooked unfed; they didn't. They looked bloated with food, mother, father and remaining two children. Perhaps the mother was really the worst and you only noticed the others were fat because she impressed fatness on you.

'Anyway it's a good thing you caught us,' said Mrs Boyle, swallowing a mouthful of cake, 'because we're moving right away. We've had enough.'

'You going far?'

'Rugby. Fred's got a job there. We want to get out of this. Shirley's gone. We won't see her again. I don't know where she is, or where she went, or why it happened to us, but staying here's making it worse, not better. Isn't it, Fred?' She turned fiercely to her husband.

'It didn't seem right to go at first,' said Fred Boyle. 'I thought about Shirley coming home and trying to get into the house and finding fresh faces here and I couldn't bear it. But now, well, I don't think she'll come back.'

'I know she won't,' said his wife, still fierce. 'And I've had enough of the police coming round asking questions that don't do any good.'

'I'm sorry about that,' said Joan Eames apologetically.

'They're only doing their job, Eileen.'

'Oh yes, I know that. Once a month one of them comes in, just to see how we're doing,' said Eileen Boyle in savage tones.

'Oh yes, who's that?' said Joan. It was news to her.

'Coffin. That's his unlikely name. He's a high-up.'

'Yes,' said Joan. She had a strange picture of Coffin doggedly calling on this family every month and getting nothing for it.

'I think it's good of him,' said Fred Boyle suddenly.

Eileen Boyle shrugged. 'Good *for* him. It's helping him feel better. It isn't doing much for me.'

She went back to the table and sat down. 'And now what do you want?' she said to Joan.

'I suppose you could say I've come instead of him.' It had just struck Joan that this was what she was doing.

'Yes, that's what I thought. Well, take your pick. Have a look at us. Ask what you want.'

'What does he usually ask?' said Joan apologetically.

'He asks how we are. I'll tell you to save you the trouble. We're fine. Fine. Saving always that we had two daughters and now we've only got one and that this time last year I weighed eight stone and now look at me. I suppose I'm about eleven and still putting it on.' She glared at Joan. 'I can't stop eating, you see. It's a syndrome, that's what the doctor said. A shock syndrome. I've got that instead of a daughter.'

'Eileen!' said her husband.

'Poor old Shirley,' said the other daughter who had kept quiet until now. She was a tiny plump child, a mature ten-year-old who had the world as well weighed up now as she would have when she was eighty. 'She was a trouble when she was here and it's worse now she's gone.'

'Julie!' said her mother.

140

'You said yourself what a trouble she was,' said Julie. 'Ever so often. I don't think Shirl liked it!'

'No child is ever a trouble to her mother,' said Eileen Boyle.

'Well, she was to you. Or she certainly thought she was.'

'Now you're making that up. You want to show off in front of this lady.'

A screaming irresistible desire to say I'm no lady, I'm a policewoman, came to Joan Eames.

'She thought you didn't like her, Mum,' said Julie. '"Mum doesn't like me as much as you." She often said it. After you'd had a row.'

'We never had rows.'

Julie shrugged.

'Do you think she ran away from home because she was unhappy?' said Joan Eames bluntly.

'No. Never,' said Mrs Boyle. 'She'd have come home, of course she'd have come home. You mustn't take any notice of what Julie says. The quarrels we had didn't matter. They were just in the family.'

'Was she what you'd call a lonely child?' said Joan Eames.

'No one's lonely in this family,' asserted Mrs Boyle. 'No one.'

'Everyone's lonely sometimes,' said Fred Boyle, surprisingly.

'Not what I call lonely,' said his wife.

'Would you say Shirley was what anyone else would call lonely?' said Joan Eames patiently. She had begun to see there might be a pattern in the answers she would get from the families of the missing children.

'They all go around in a little gang these kids,' said Mrs Boyle. 'They're never on their own.'

Joan looked at Julie. 'All her class at school were friends with Shirley,' said Julie uneasily. 'She didn't know many in my lot, though.' The generation gap started at zero.

The next house Joan Eames went to, the home of Grace Parker who had disappeared on April 23, had all the curtains drawn in the front of the house. Quietly Joan walked round the garden path to where she could see the back windows. The curtains were all drawn here too. The flowers in the small garden were neglected and the grass was rank.

It looked hopeless to try but she went round to the front door again and knocked. There was no answer, so she raised the letter box and peered inside. Here too all was still and quiet, but she didn't think the Parkers were away all the same.

She could see a bottle of milk standing on a table and the post had been picked up and put beside it. Not opened though, nothing had been opened. Over the weeks a pile of letters had grown up there and been left untouched.

She drew a deep breath and turned away.

A woman was staring at her from over the fence. Oh yes, there's always a neighbour, Joan thought, who knows more than you think she does and yet less than she imagines.

'You won't get no answer,' she said. 'They never answer.'

'They are there, then?'

She nodded. 'You can't blame them. Didn't happen straight away. Seemed to come on gradually. He goes to work, you know. Comes out and goes to work. He does the shopping too. Well, they've got to live. But you never see *her*.'

142

'How long since you've seen her?'

'Not since just after . . . you know what I mean. Just *after*. I don't like to say it aloud. Such a pity too. Such a nice bright little girl. The only one, too. It's always worse then, isn't it?'

Joan dug around for the little nugget of information this woman might yet possess.

'It's been bad for you too,' she began.

'Yes. You can't get away from it, you see.'

'No one can,' agreed Joan Eames.

'Oh some can, don't you worry, some can shut their minds to it and go on just as before. I could name you some names and not far away from here, either. But I'm not like that.'

'I couldn't be, either.'

'Yes, well, for you it's your job, isn't it?' said the woman sharply. 'You never knew her. But I knew that little girl from the minute she was born. Of course, she was a late comer, they'd been married twenty years and I don't think they knew what to make of this little one when she came. I often used to think she felt out in the cold.'

'Oh, you did?'

'Yes. When she first came they used to look at her as if she was a little changeling. They were close to each other and sort of shut her out. Oh, it happens. You can understand it.' She lowered her voice. 'But I reckon they feel it now and it's preying on them and that's why . . . ' she nodded her head towards the windows. 'That's why *that*.'

Joan Eames looked up at the darkened windows. She was almost sure she saw a curtain move.

'They're watching.'

'Yes, they do that. I suppose they want to know what's going on outside. Goodness knows what goes on inside that house. I've lived beside them all these years and I don't know them. But the child was friendly enough, poor little soul. Too friendly for her own good.'

'Well, thanks for telling me.'

'I thought the police had given up coming around,' said the woman, watching her walk away. 'But you're police, aren't you?'

'We never quite give up,' said Joan as she went. 'Sometimes it looks like it, that's all.'

Finally she tried the family of Katherine Gable in Archangel Street. They were the easiest of all the families to interview, the most normal and yet the saddest.

They simply didn't undertand what had happened to them. One of their number was gone and the rest of the family huddled together for protection like cattle in a storm. They were all at home when she got there, all crowded into one small room, all six of them. She looked round at them. The average IQ in the Gable family wasn't very high, but they were *good*. You could tell that with just one look. The second look showed you that something had crept into the family tree a generation or so ago, some mutation which had survived and marked them all. They were all little people with somewhat oversized heads, hands and feet. Nothing spectacular, they were not monsters, but once you were conscious of it you were very conscious of it. Joan Eames found herself trying not to look. Mr and Mrs Gable both had the same appearance and must have been blood relations.

They were not very articulate and Joan Eames did not talk to them much although she tried to follow John Coffin's instructions and observe them sharply. She stayed with them only a short time, thinking to herself that it was now only evening and she had fulfilled her task well within the time allowed her. Tomorrow probably she could go back to her routine baby-minding jobs.

She could see they were glad when she rose to go. They all got up too, father, mother, son and three daughters and the sole representative of an earlier generation, Gran.

Gran only spoke as Joan was leaving. 'Katherine's not one of us,' was all she said. Then suddenly added: 'She's more of a Holden, that's my husband's side. Yes, Katherine's a Holden.'

'Could I see a photograph of Katherine, please?' Joan asked. One of the things that embarrassed her in the interview with the Gables was the way they hurried to do what she asked, open the door, pull out a chair, answer a question and bring a photograph. It made her want to say please and thank you hard all the time.

'Thank you.' She looked at the photograph. It was a school group, Katherine with some other friends, one child had an arm round her waist and another smiled at her, she must have been a popular girl. Joan saw at once why Katherine wasn't one with the rest of the family. She was a tall thin wiry child with a keen gaze. Physically she was utterly different. Mentally, too, probably. She handed the photograph back. 'Thank you. I see what you mean.'

She went back to Coffin who made time for her out of a morass of other duties and who listened to her while looking out of the window. But he listened carefully and took it all in.

'Good girl. You seem to have understood what I wanted.'

'I think I did.' He didn't work at his marriage any more was the phrase someone had used, but he didn't attract her on this account, the way he would have done some girls she knew.

'Oh you did. You got out what I really wanted: that the missing girls could all have been looking for affection.'

'Yes,' said Joan Eames. 'Love from a stranger.'

'And you got the other thing too.'

'The other thing?'

'Yes.' He grinned at her. 'The fact that they all had friends.'

'I began to see the point of that.'

'Of course you did. And the other thing: the adult figure who must have known them all. There's more than one, of course, but there's one who begins to stand out. And now you can go out and see the other girl.'

'The other girl?'

'The one who came back. Kim Simpson of Riga Street. Number 3 Riga Street, I believe. Actually it's the first house. Number 1 is a shop. She went off on Boxing Day, but she came back.'

'So she isn't really one of ours?'

'I'm not so sure. I think she's one of the dark number. The crimes we never get to hear about until too late.'

'Only she wasn't really a crime.'

'We don't know, do we?' said Coffin. 'Go and have a word with her. Get more out of her than anyone else has. See what she has to say.'

It was getting late in the day to see what Kim Simpson had to say, but Joan Eames thought it might be worth trying. Children didn't go to bed so early round here.

As soon as she saw Kim (who characteristically opened the door herself) she recognized her for what she was, one of those sharp little London sparrows. She was so sharp that you knew she would end up cutting herself; you also knew that she would never see this coming. She trusted in her own shrewdness to the death. She would

146

die with her eyes open, not believing in what she saw. Joan Eames thought she was lucky to have got home in one piece.

'Hello.' She met Joan's eye with self assurance. 'Heard you were going around. Wondered if you'd be in to see me.' She let Joan walk into the house. 'Well, you didn't think you were a secret, did you?'

She led the way into the small sitting-room. 'Sit down and make yourself at home. Mum's out and Dad's in the kitchen.'

'Better call him in.'

'I won't eat you. And I don't think you'll eat me.'

'He has to be here while I talk to you.'

'Yeah. I know what you coppers are like. Always watching each other. If you and I have a little talk alone then they might start saying *things* about you.' She went to the door and called. 'Dad! here, Dad.' She came back. 'He comes if you call him.'

'Yes. I can hear.'

'I wouldn't. Someone call me like that and I'd just sit. That's me.' She didn't hate herself.

'I suppose he gets used to walking,' said Kim, sitting down and crossing her ankles.

Contradicting the build-up which his daughter, whether unconsciously or not, had given him as a bullied man, Robert Simpson was trim and bright-eyed, very like the girl, and with a mind of his own. Joan Eames recognized him as a local postman.

'Take no notice of her, miss,' he said. 'We didn't beat her enough when she was young. But she's a good girl.' And he looked at her with affection and she looked the same way back.

'I'd like to ask her a few questions about what happened on Boxing Day.'

'But there was nothing in that. She was a naughty girl and went off to the fair and came home late, but that was all. We know it.'

'But you reported her missing to the police.'

'That was before she came back. All right, we got anxious, but she came home.'

'Where did you go, Kim?' said Joan softly.

'To the fairground. You know, the one down at the Blue.' The Blue was what everyone locally called the stretch of wide street opposite the Blue Anchor public house. Weekdays it held stalls and street market. There was also this small fairground owned by Mr Di Finzio.

'And as well as that?'

'Nowhere else. I stayed there. I went on things. I lost my sense of time.' She was glib.

'Did you do anything else?' Joan was digging around.

'No.' She was prompt.

'Not anything? Not even get yourself a drink? They sell orange juice and such, don't they?'

'I had an ice-cream.' She seemed slow about that one.

'Just one?'

'I had more than one.'

'How long were you gone?'

Kim shrugged.

Joan Eames looked at Mr Simpson, sitting there taking his ease. Like father like daughter. 'How long was she gone? When did you report her missing?'

'She left the house around three. We ate late that day. We got anxious any time after six. It was a cold wet night and she ought to have been in. We reported her missing at eight. She came in around ten. Naughty girl, eh?' He looked at her fondly.

'It seems a long time to have been doing not very much,' said Joan exasperated.

Kim's eyes, bright, alert, amused, rested on her.

She's like a little tiger, thought Joan, roaming through the London forest, sure it can eat before it gets eaten. But even little tigers meet bigger tigers.

'All right,' she said, rising. 'You were in your ice-cream heaven and you didn't notice anything.'

Kim blinked.

Chapter Thirteen

The ice-cream van did its daily tour through the streets of the district on the next day. Cyrus was a good driver and salesman, if a bored one. The job, he knew, was beneath him, but it gave him time for thought. Cyrus always had problems to think about, if not of one sort, then another. Driving around and selling ice-cream gave him a chance to think about them. His main problem at the moment concerned the Club for UFO watchers. He had led a little revolution to destroy John Plowman's power in it, only to find that John had lost interest and was moving out himself. The frivolity of John's attitude infuriated him.

'He's not a serious character,' he said aloud to the steering wheel of his van. This steering wheel took a good deal of Cy's conversation and he was even beginning to see it as a sort of face that could hear and comprehend without answering back. This picture was subliminal, of course. Cy wasn't openly mad, but it was there under the skin of his mind.

He saw a group of children on their way to school standing at the street corner, but he didn't slow down near them or play his musical chime. He knew they were not going to buy. Cy was not a child lover but he had learnt a good deal about children.

It was almost two in the afternoon and the van was well on schedule. From now until school was out again was a slack time. Cy rather enjoyed his dreamy tours through the streets. Today was hot and sticky, but he felt cool enough.

'Cool cold Cyrus,' he murmured reflectively. 'In the States they'd probably be training me to drive a space vehicle. With my nerve I'm wasted here. I don't know why I don't emigrate.' To emigrate was another dream of Cy's. He didn't mind where he went. Somewhere there was a planet waiting for him.

The afternoon passed pleasantly. School came out, he sold some ice-cream. The traffic on the roads thickened as the factories and offices started to close. As it was a hot day he sold a few water-ice lollipops to adults for a change. It always gave him a feeling of triumph to sell ice-cream to a grown-up. The reason for this was buried deep inside him, but it was probably connected with the idea that he'd made them back down in front of him. Made them show appeasement signals, as his friend Tony Young would have said. Aggression and appeasement were nicely mingled in Cyrus. He would have made an awkward emigrant. Except on an empty planet. But of course that was what he was really looking for.

He continued his course, monotonous to some, but not to him. Saxe-Coburg Street together with Riga Street and Archangel Street were like lines on a children's game. He went up one and down the other. Down Riga Street, turn left into Saxe-Coburg Street, right turn and up Riga Street. Through Riga Street, then a more complex set of roads, including Harper Road where Tony Young lived and back to where you started. There were short cuts between the roads for children and cats.

He was almost finished for the day now. He drove on as steadily as possible, stopping where he must, selling as demands met him. He was a little jumpy. No one's nerves were quite steady in this district just now.

One of his friends, a man who kept a shop, hailed him and asked for a tub of chocolate ice-cream. Cyrus didn't really like one of his friends to stop him and order. The truth was he felt his job was beneath him and he didn't care for them to see him at it.

'We're out of chocolate,' he said, although there was an unopened container of it in the back of the freezer that he had placed there himself. He was driving around in his candy coloured van well supplied with chocolate ice-cream but he felt like not selling it.

'Strawberry, then.'

'Yes, we have strawberry,' he admitted reluctantly.

'I don't mind. I don't like ice-cream. But my wife's away and I have to eat *something*.'

'You could drink some milk.'

Cy's friend did not answer this point, but it confirmed his idea that Cy would never make a salesman. At any rate, not of ice-cream.

'Your wife on holiday?'

'No. No holiday. She just took the children away. You can't blame her.'

'No.' Cyrus considered. His own wife had not gone and wouldn't be going.

'She's worried for the children. She's been worked up for months. But when the last disappearance happened, she really got worried.'

'You're dropping the ice-cream down your shirt.'

'Well, it's a bad business. You got any theories?'

'Yes. One theory,' said Cyrus.

'What's that?'

'That we won't ever find out who did it.'

He started up the van and drove off, leaving his friend standing on the kerb with his ice-cream in his hand somehow feeling naked.

'Cyrus,' he called out angrily, 'next time you ask me if

you can leave your van in my yard, I'll say go and buy some ice-cream.'

Cyrus drove to the depot where he was due to check in the van. He was a little early, but on such a day it seemed more sensible to be early than late. In any case, he knew how to time it so that his earliness slid in unnoticed.

He was whistling melodiously. He enjoyed music.

As he passed the corner of Palliser Road where the old stables stood he saw an ambulance draw up. Then another. He drove very, very slowly, watching. This was the stable where Tom Butt's body had been found.

Cyrus stopped whistling, and hurried on. He thought it might be a night to be home.

Chapter Fourteen

'Yes, you did well with Kim Simpson,' said Coffin, offering a compliment to Joan Eames that same evening. 'What did you make of her?'

'She's a bloody little liar,' said Joan dispassionately.

'Yes. That's what everyone else said. Any idea why she's lying?'

'I don't know. She might just be stupid.'

'She would have to have a certain kind of reason for not saying anything. I don't think in the case of Kim Simpson we need use the word loyalty.'

'It'll be a boy. Something male,' said Joan Eames.

'A local boy, do you think?'

'Yes. Probably. Because she'd have to get to know him. And *he'd* have to be a liar too.'

Coffin nodded. 'I agree.'

'Because he's kept it all quiet,' she said.

'A local boy who's a liar,' said Coffin.

'And she's only twelve. So he has to be a little boy. Or one with junior tastes.'

'A local boy who tells lies and has a taste for little girls. Any suggestions?'

Joan Eames looked at him brightly but did not say anything.

'We have candidates,' said Coffin. 'We have candidates.'

He let Joan Eames go and she met Sergeant Parr on her way out. She still liked the look of him. After her recent work she liked the look of him better than ever.

He seemed so clean and normal. Also she strongly suspected she was a little brighter and cleverer than he was, and that too seemed highly desirable.

However, he didn't seem to have an eye for her. He walked right past her with a friendly smile. She couldn't pretend that everything started to spin for him when he saw her.

He did indeed smile at her because he thought she was a nice girl and a hard worker. Moreover, she seemed to have the ear of his boss, Coffin, at the moment. She was not, however, all that alluring and on no account was he going to marry a policewoman.

He was in a hurry, as Joan Eames saw. Something was up, but no one so far had told her what.

'Boss there?' he said, nodding at the door.

'I've just left him. What's doing?'

'We found something. And this is definitely it.'

'Does *he* know?' She nodded towards the door.

'Oh yeah, he knows.'

'He didn't say anything.'

Parr shrugged. 'You know him.'

'I'm beginning to.' She continued on her way out.

Coffin looked up as Parr came into his room. 'Well?'

'Two bodies, sir. So far.'

'Think there'll be more?'

'Oh yes.'

'The lot?'

Parr nodded.

'You don't look too well.'

'It's not nice, sir.'

'No.' Coffin considered. 'Tell Dove I'll be round. You go back. Keep everyone else out.'

'There's a crowd outside already.'

'Keep everyone out. I'll be coming.'

After Parr had gone, Coffin got one of the tapes he had taken from Tony Young and played it. He didn't listen to all of it, but selected certain passages which he had marked. He felt very sad and very puzzled as he listened. This was Tony Young's tape and a lot had to be explained away about it.

Since the discovery of Tom Butt's body the police team had been quietly and methodically going over the stables inch by inch. Progress had been slow. In fact at first it hadn't looked like progress at all, but an endless monotonous turning over of rubbish to no real purpose. Two detective constables were specially assigned to the job.

They had got through the front stables and were working on the two that lay at the back of the cobbled yard when the character of their work changed.

They were silent about it at first, working away without a word. It seemed too important what they might be now approaching, to make a shout about it.

Even when one of them spoke it was in a very quiet voice. 'Does it look the way to you it does to me?'

'I think so.'

'This is really it, isn't it?'

Later on, in making his first report, the detective constable repeated this phrase and it got picked up by Sergeant Parr and passed on as the way to put it. This was really it.

Just then, though, they worked on for a few more minutes, moving very slowly, sorting through the piles of lumber and rubbish in front of them.

'I knew as soon as I saw that girl's shoe we were coming to something,' said one of them suddenly. 'And then the way the things are stacked on the floor here. Artificial. Contrived.'

156

'It had a smell,' said the other bluntly.

His companion made a sick noise.

'Steady. Help me shift this packing case.'

'Look at that.' In this part of the stables the floor was old, old brick. But someone had disturbed the neat herring-bone pattern. 'A rotten job. Not put back carefully.'

'Shall we dig?'

For answer, the senior man of the two prised up a loose brick and moved the soil underneath with the tip of his shoe. It was loose. He crouched down and put his face towards the soil. Then he stood up. 'Yes, that's the smell. Wait here. I'm going to telephone.'

He moved towards the door.

So this was what Coffin knew when he spoke to Joan Eames and didn't tell her anything: he knew that this time they really had something. After speaking with Parr, he knew that the bodies of two girls had been discovered. He also grasped the probability that more would be found.

Shirley Boyle, March 18 of last year.

Grace Parker, April 23, this year.

Katherine Gable, June 26, this year.

Thus went the roll call. And then there was the last name of all, Belle Anderson, this year, this month, this week.

Later that night the police found the body of a third girl. So far there had been only tentative identification but this child was thought to be Katherine Gable.

They had already found the little bag that Shirley Boyle was carrying and the shoe worn by Grace Parker; and this third child had a red necklace still round her throat.

'So no one went up in a space ship,' said Coffin. 'And the man who killed Tom Butt killed the children.'

'Man?'

'Whoever it was,' corrected Coffin irritably.

'But why kill Butt?'

'Because the killer was frightened. Butt knew something. Perhaps saw something. It's likely.'

'D'you think Butt was in on it? A helper?'

'No. No, there's no evidence of that. Butt shows all the signs of being innocent. Innocent and unlucky. He was that sort.'

'And the girls?'

'They were the sort to be victims,' said Coffin grimly. 'It was written all over them. Don't you see it? There ought to be classes in the identification of victims for all policemen. Then we might get them before they become victims.'

'Too late for these,' said Dove. 'And anyway, no one ever thinks of himself as a victim.'

'We have too many madmen in this district.'

'Not all of them are murderers.'

'But this one is.'

'We know more or less where to look, don't we?'

'Well, yes. The girls, as well as being natural born victims, had one thing in common.'

'They all lived round here.'

'More specific than that. They all went to the same school.'

'Naturally.'

'Not naturally. There's the Church School up at St Michael's. One of them could have gone to the Sisters there. Or there's the new school down Tanner Lane, but no, they all went to the same school.'

'Which is the nearest.'

'It's the nearest. And as well as going to the same school, they were the same age. Give or take a bit. And they were all bright. Clever girls. They have streaming at that school according to ability: A, B or C. They were all A.'

'I'm against it,' said Dove mechanically.

'Me too. I was always B myself. But they were all in the A stream, clever bright little victims, and they were taught for the last year by the same teacher: that is they had the same class teacher, Jean Young.'

'They all knew Jean Young.'

'Yes. She's friendly. Well liked. She had them in to see her sometimes, took them on expeditions at the weekend. She's a local girl. Grew up round here and she doesn't forget it.'

'She's a nice girl.'

'So they all knew her well. And her home. And her brother.'

'And he knew them.'

'Yes. Tony Young knew every one of those girls. And that's what I don't like.'

'We'll get him in. We can have a nice long talk.'

'He won't say anything.'

'Not at first,' said Dove ominously. Coffin looked at him. Dove had a certain rough reputation for getting what he wanted. You wouldn't think it to look at him.

They waited. Soon it became clear that they had found three bodies and three was all.

'It's not quite enough, is it?'

'The Anderson girl?'

'Yes, Belle Anderson. We don't have her yet. Where is she?'

'Another affair altogether?' said Dove uneasily.

'Two abductors? I hope not. I really hope not.'

'You always get imitators.'

'I want to find that Anderson child. I want her soon.'

'We'll get Tony Young in,' said Dove. Not soothingly, the position was hardly one on which to be soothing, but certainly in a placatory way. 'With any luck we'll get a lead from him.'

'It's taking a lot for granted.'

'He's in it somewhere, I swear.'

'Yes.' Coffin considered. 'He is. I know you can shake anything out of anyone.' He said it, not with approval, but more with the air of making an admission. As a matter of fact, it wasn't one he usually made. It was on the dark side of his life, this sort of thing, something he was not explicit about. You dealt in violence. You learnt how to use it. But sometimes there was a kick-back. A little while ago he had been almost crazy, and might be again. 'If it's there.'

'It is with him. I swear it.'

'There's someone else who can help us.'

Dove looked up.

'Kim Simpson. If things don't move soon, I'll get Kim Simpson and I'll shake the truth out of her.'

Chapter Fifteen

Judith came back into Tony Young's life in the same off-hand manner that she had departed. She was waiting for him in her white car outside the shop where he was working. She opened the car door silently and he got in and sat beside her.

'Word's been getting round to me,' she said, 'that you're in trouble.'

'I could be,' said Tony, who didn't like to think about it. He had given up thinking these days. Packed his bags and moved from his mind, leaving it empty. Being empty, it echoed a good deal.

'You're a boy with education. Why don't you do something about it?'

'I didn't want to,' said Tony, with truth. 'Frightened.'

'You're a clever boy, too. Why did you let yourself get into this mess?' She was scolding him, her face was serious, she really wanted to know.

'I didn't want to get caught up,' said Tony, not answering her directly. 'Not like Jean. She's in it. I thought if the institutions don't exist to suit me, then I'll make them. I was doing it, too.'

'You can meet a lot of lunatics that way,' said Judith, dispassionately. 'And you have.'

'How did you get to be so much wiser and more worldly than me?'

'This is no time to get funny.'

'It's not so much of a joke.'

'You need me to prove you're human.'

'Let's start with a little club, shall we? Just you and me. And the car,' he added, patting it. There was strength in the feel of it and he began to look more cheerful.

'I think I take it back: you're not human.'

He took her hand. 'I'm human.'

They sat for a moment in silence.

'Am I holding the hand of a murderer?'

'What do you think?'

'I think not.'

'I'd like to believe I'm not,' he said.

She took her hand away. 'Don't you *know*?'

'Well, in a way.'

'That's good: in a way! How many ways are there?'

'You have had an easy life,' he said jeeringly, 'if you think it's only the things you know with your mind that are the real things. Even I know better than that.'

She started the car and drove slowly through the streets. There was plenty of traffic.

'Tell me,' she said.

'I noticed long ago that the kids always seemed to take off on the night our club was out at a sighting. Could be just coincidence. Or, if you thought flying saucers were landing then you could think perhaps the saucermen were collecting them.'

'I don't believe in those saucermen.'

'Some people do. For instance, I had a letter from old Miss Jones to say she's reasonably certain there's been a saucer hovering over her ward in the hospital.'

'That would worry me!'

'It's bucked her up. But I don't have to believe. I don't have to say, yes, I believe. I just ran the set-up. But I was always out the nights the children went. I was bound to ask myself if that meant anything.'

'Are you telling me you're out of your mind?'

162

'I have a tape recorder. I use it to put my thoughts in order. One night I played it and there was a child's voice on it.'

'I'd like to hear it.'

He looked out of the window. They were still in Saxe-Coburg Street. 'You can't do that,' he said. 'When I tried to play it again, there was silence.'

'Yes, I see your trouble,' said Judith. 'You don't remember doing *anything* yourself?'

Tony shook his head.

'Then there's nothing there,' said Judith. 'I don't believe in amnesia.'

'Good.'

He didn't sound very cheerful. Judith glanced at him and drove more quickly. At the park gate, under the trees, she stopped.

'You're hiding something from me, aren't you?'

'Not exactly hiding. More keeping it to myself.'

'Show me the difference.'

'If I'm using my own judgement, then that's keeping it to myself. If I'm just frightened to tell, then that's hiding it.'

'You certainly do talk a lot.' She was half amused, half exasperated. Not quite serious yet, but beginning to be worried for him. She was a girl who had a capacity to love and protect.

'There seemed blood on my shirt when I got home the night the last child was missing. Fresh blood it was. Jean found it there.'

'Jean's a disinterested person, I take it?'

'Jean has no loves and no hates. She's never found anything to inspire her to love. She's still looking.'

'She might not be so fond of you as you think. She might not mind to see you hop.'

'No, I don't think so.'

'They've not found that Anderson child, Tony.'

'I wish they may,' said Tony.

'There's enough substance in this to make it a real nightmare.'

'Jude, if I was a real murderer, I'd have a good cover story, wouldn't I?'

'Tony, you've got one. You're *you*.'

'Jude, if that blood was on my shirt, and I'm not a murderer, then someone put it there.'

'On purpose?' she said sceptically.

'The other thing about that blood, Judith, when I took a closer look, was that it was lipstick. Not blood but lipstick.'

'Lipstick,' cried Judith in relief.

'Not your colour. It may mean something and it may not. Who knows, Judith? I don't.'

They had circled each other's position and were ready to observe each other alertly.

Presently Judith started the car.

'Where are we going?'

'To the Blue Anchor. I'm hot and thirsty. You're going to give me some coffee.'

The street market around the Blue Anchor was getting ready to pack up and go home for the day. Judith found it easy to park her car.

'Right. Into the theatre coffee-bar.'

In the last year, the aged music hall, the Prince Regent, which had then been a cinema and then stood empty, had been revived as a repertory theatre. This was where Judith worked.

The coffee-bar, which was open all day and also until after the last performance at night, was on a mezzanine floor. Judith led the way up.

The crowd and the bustle acted like a blood transfusion on Tony. He looked round cheerfully, pushed aside a young man trying to get to a table and seated himself and Judith there instead.

'I prefer a stool at the bar really,' she said.

'More private here.' He came back with two mugs of coffee. 'Here, sip this. Filthy stuff. Don't know how they have the face to make you pay for it.'

'Got to make a profit somewhere,' said Judith, sipping her coffee and looking around. 'We don't make it out of the audience, I can tell you. They jib at paying more than two and nine to see us act. And we're a *good* company.'

'Yes, I know you are. But the trouble is, publicity-wise, you're not *organized*.' Judith looked at him sharply. 'Yes, you need a bit of help there.' He leaned back comfortably. 'I've had my eye on you for some time.'

'They're a tough bunch here. Lay off them.'

'Boys, my dear, boys.' He leaned forward and suddenly looked very young. 'Anyway I wouldn't mind being an actor. I think it might be just what I'm looking for. What about it, Jude, think there's room for me?'

'You'd have to go away and learn to act,' said Judith, putting on her professional face.

'I could learn on my feet.'

'Ha, ha!'

A young man strolled over from the table by the window. 'Hello, Judith.' He stared at Tony.

'Hello, Alan.' The two young men looked at each other appraisingly. 'Alan Riddell, Tony Young,' said Judith hurriedly. 'Tony wants to work for us. Anything going?'

'I think we want someone to help shift the scenery round the back,' said Alan.

'What job would that be called?' asked Tony, who knew that titles and status were deeply intertwined.

'Assistant stage manager.'

'Any chance of doing a bit of acting?'

Alan shrugged.

Tony made up his mind. 'I'll take it.'

'I'll speak to Tommy Titmus.'

'Who's he?'

'He's the SM,' said Judith.

'He's a tough little man with big muscles,' said Alan.

'Got any interests has he? Tell me the sort of thing he's interested in outside work?'

'He's just a tough little man with big muscles. I don't think he reads and he's not colour blind. Don't try to infiltrate *him*.'

Tony was silent.

'Come over to my table and meet Joey.'

'Who's Joey?'

'She's writing us a play,' said Alan, leading the way to the table by the window. 'Aren't you, Joey? Aren't you writing us a play?'

Joey was tall and thin with a thick wave of pale hair falling over her left eye. The right eye was bright and observant. 'Yes,' said Joey.

'And it's going to be finished ten light years from now because Joey's a slow worker, aren't you, Joey?'

'Yes,' said Joey.

'Shove over, Joey, so we can all sit down.'

'Yes,' said Joey, hardly moving.

'What's it about, your play?' asked Tony.

Joey looked at him wordlessly, but he thought that her lips faintly mouthed her favourite word. Yes.

'Her dialogue's her strong point,' said Alan.

From where they sat they could see the street in the evening light. As they sat there Coffin was in the old

166

stables surveying the bodies of the dead girls. This was what time was like: one and indivisible.

Alan looked at his watch.

'Yes,' said Judith. 'You'd better get going, Tony. I start work soon.'

'What is it this week?'

'Oh, I'm just walking on. But I'm understudying the lead.'

'She won't be ill,' said Alan.

'Not her,' said Judith. 'She'd go on if her head had been cut off.'

'You'd hardly know the difference sometimes.'

'It'd be more pleasant. I love her, though.'

'I know you do, darling,' said Alan.

As they sat there they heard an ambulance come through the street. They looked and saw another following it. A black police car followed.

'Looks bad,' said Alan.

'I heard they'd found something,' said Judith uneasily.

'Those poor kids,' said Alan. 'I hope they catch the monster. It's spoiling our business round here.' He stood up and went to look farther out of the window. 'They'll get him anyway. I bet they could put a finger on him now. Well, it's clear, isn't it? It has to be someone the kids knew. It has to be a friend of the family.'

'Think so?' said Judith.

'Yes, sure. You wait and see. Coming?'

'Yes,' said Joey. She stood up. She was wearing a ground length blue coat and black pointed shoes.

'She's a bit Gothic, isn't she?' said Tony as Alan followed her out. 'I bet there's a lot of silence in her dialogue.'

Alan and Joey had disappeared. Judith and Tony stood

on the street, looking at each other. 'Time for young lovers,' said Tony.

'I'm really terrified for you, my darling,' said Judith.

Tony made an inarticulate noise.

'Don't mind my language,' she said softly.

'Can I borrow your car?' said Tony. 'I believe if I could drive in your car then I'd feel braver.'

'Well, all right.' She gave him the keys. 'But bring it back tomorrow.'

He got in, started the engine and waved his hand. 'A la Bastille.' She raised her hand in salute. 'Oh look, there's Dave. Without his girl friend.'

Dave was walking slowly along the road.

Tony caught him up.

'Hallo there, Dave.'

'Hello, friend.'

'You don't look pleased to see me.'

'I was thinking.' He looked at the car. 'That yours?'

'Belongs to my girl. Where's your girl, Dave? The one I never see.'

'She's shy. That's why.'

'So you say.'

'You don't believe in her?'

'Half and half, Dave boy. She's not a friend of the family.'

'You're blocking the traffic with that car that isn't yours,' said Dave spitefully. Tony knew he was jealous about the car. The more so as he was a good driver himself, when he got the chance.

The ice-cream van moved slowly past them, a uniformed figure pretending not to see them.

'There goes Cy,' said his brother-in-law. 'Is he in trouble at home!'

'What trouble?'

168

'I dunno. Quarrel, quarrel, quarrel, that's all it is.'

'Still using his tape recorder?'

'He hasn't done so much with that lately,' said Dave after a pause.

'You still watching him?'

'I do what I can. See you later, Tony. I'm off to see my girl.'

He hurried away. But he hated talking about his brother-in-law, of whom he was really frightened, and when he met his girl he found himself unable to talk to her much. He had promised himself to be really gay for her tonight, to really sparkle. But he could only mumble a few shy words.

'Hello, my dear,' he said. 'Here's the ice-cream you wanted. It's the sort you like, isn't it? I got it from Cy's van. Perhaps I shouldn't say this . . . ' He hesitated. 'But keep away from Cy, will you?' he licked his own ice-cream, it was chocolate. 'Good ice-cream? Do you know he beat me once? He said it was to punish me, but I think it was because he wanted to.

'And the other person you can keep away from is Tony Young. I can't tell you all, now, but he's a bad, bad boy.'

Chapter Sixteen

The police, too, were thinking about Tony Young. It seemed to Coffin that his figure was pushing up from the background of the case and quietly trying to assert its identity. This is what a murderer should always fear, that his features will show up, hide them how he will. And there is a good reason for this. He *wants* to be found. Guilt wants to shout. This is why he leaves behind the things that count. Clues, so called. Clues are just bits of himself that he has left behind as he passes through the scene.

At this moment the person the police most wanted to talk to was Kim Simpson.

'What, now?' said Dove. He squinted at the clock. By now it was close on midnight.

'No.' Coffin considered. 'Much as I'd like to drag her out of bed, we can't do it. She's a tricky enough customer already, that girl. We have to be very, very careful with her. No, we won't get her up. But tomorrow, that'll be the day. Meanwhile get a message round to her mother to keep her under wraps. Tell her not to let Kim out. I want her where I can see her.'

'I'll get the word round.'

He sent Joan Eames. She had a terse few words with Kim's hostile and sleepy mother.

'Keep Kim home?' she said crossly. 'Let me tell you I always look after my girl. I'm not a careless mother.'

'Well, just keep an eye on her until my boss has seen her,' said Joan wearily; she too was tired.

'Aa,' said Mrs Simpson and shut the door with a bang.

Joan shrugged and walked away. For her the day was over. She could go home and get what rest she could.

'I'll sleep,' she thought. 'I'm so tired, I'd sleep on a pole.' She slept soundly, not even wondering what morning would bring.

For Tony Young it straightaway brought a summons to see Coffin. He was up, sleepily drinking tea in the kitchen and thinking about Judith's white car, when Parr arrived.

He saw Parr from the kitchen window and went to the door without waiting for him to knock.

'You're early,' he said. 'Jean's not up yet.'

'Let her stay that way. Where's your father?'

'Gone to work. I suppose you want me to come with you? You came early to be sure of getting me home. Weren't you running a risk?'

'I knew you were home.'

'How? Been watching the house all night?'

Parr was silent.

Tony walked to the window. 'Or else you thought I'd never go and leave that car behind. Or you thought that Jean would let you know if I walked out. Is that it? Some little arrangement with Jean? You'd be a fool to trust to that. Jean loves me.'

'I knew you wouldn't go away.'

'It's more than I did,' said Tony, putting on his coat. 'Know something? I nearly got in that car and drove into the night. But I didn't. I wanted to come home. Can you beat it? I was a tired boy and I wanted to come home. I should have kept running years ago.'

He drank his tea and put the cup and saucer neatly on the table. 'I'm ready then.'

'Better leave a note for Jean.'

'You think she'll enjoy getting a note from me saying I've been nicked?'

Parr said: 'Go up and say it to her then.' For some minutes he had been conscious of sounds from upstairs. He shifted nervously. He knew Jean was going to beat him to it and she did.

'Hello,' she said, from the door. 'Creeping out?'

'We hoped you wouldn't hear. We didn't want to disturb you.'

'Some voices I always hear,' Jean said.

'Go back to bed, Jean,' said her brother.

'It's not wise to go out without some breakfast,' she said in a calm voice.

'I don't have much choice.'

'I'll get him something to eat down at the station. If he wants it.'

'Jean, I couldn't eat a thing.' At the door, he turned and said, 'Will you stand by me, Jean?'

'Yes,' she said in a level voice.

Parr made an excuse to go back to her. 'Did you mean that? About standing by him? It might not be easy.'

'I don't know,' said Jean, still in the same even tone from which she had not deviated this day. 'I don't know what it might mean to him. But this doesn't seem the time for speaking the absolute truth. Not for me. Not for you. And probably not for him either.'

Parr still stood there looking at her.

'Better go,' she said, 'or Tony'll be crying out for you.'

She watched them get into the police car and drive away. Not to her surprise she saw that her neighbours in Harper Road were watching too. She resisted the temptation to poke her tongue out at them, and marched inside to get her breakfast.

Tony was braver than he looked, and he arrived in John

Coffin's office with composure. At least he had slept that night, so compared with the detectives in the room he looked rested.

'You arresting me?'

'No.'

'Then why am I here?'

'You're always so dramatic, Tony,' observed John Coffin mildly. 'Arrest's too big a word. I wanted to talk with you. I asked you to come to talk and you came.'

'Yes, that was good of me,' agreed Tony, 'but I really didn't have a lot of choice.'

'I wanted to have a look at you.'

'Look, then. Here I am. Am I what you want?'

'That's what I don't know yet. I have a picture of a person in my mind and I want to see if you match up to it.'

'That doesn't sound sensible talk.'

'Oh, it's sensible.'

'And is it a nice face you're trying to match me up to?'

'I'm not sure about the features, yet,' said Coffin, watching him. 'But I'll describe the person I'm looking for.'

'That sounds imaginative.'

'No, not imaginative. And I've had some help.' He glanced at Dove, Parr and a third silent detective. 'It's something we built up together.' Then he looked back to Tony. 'Sit down and make yourself comfortable.'

'I'm comfortable.' But he didn't look it.

'This is the person I'm looking for! A man, not old. Perhaps younger than we think, but age not quite clear.'

'Say ageless,' said Tony.

'You could say that. I would prefer to say a young or youngish man. Secondly he's local. He comes from this district.'

'Sure about that?'

'Yes, sure. He crawls out of the woodwork round here and knows his way about it. He knows the smell of the place and what's more the place knows him. He doesn't stand out.'

'A youngish local funny?' said Tony.

'I bet he looks quite normal.'

'He sounds really nice.'

'I think a few people like him. Women probably do. There'll be a motherly figure in the background all right.'

'I don't know anyone like this person you're describing.'

'Well, let me continue a bit longer. Add a few more details. The motherly thing, now that isn't just guessing. Someone must be covering up for this character. Deliberately not noticing signs on his clothing, disturbance of manner, even absences. That sounds like a woman. And a woman in a close relationship. Say a mother, wife or sister.'

'I like that bit about close relationships,' said Tony through white lips, 'because to me it sounds as though this character can't have close relationships. Especially with women.'

'Not adult relationships. Childish ones, though. Immature relationships.'

Coffin waited for a minute as if expecting Tony to say something, and then went on: 'He can come and go as he wants, this fellow I'm thinking about. So he's probably known to have outside interests. His family don't remark on him being out a lot. Or if they do then they know how to keep quiet about it. He's clever, I should think. Yes, I think we're all agreed he's a person of some intelligence. He may be quite good at covering this intelligence up. I suppose you're thinking that's not like *you*, Tony?'

'I've been trying not to think about it in relationship with me.'

Coffin smiled, and went on: 'Still, you can't help thinking about it a bit, can you, Tony? Now the other thing we know about this person is that he's probably not too strong physically. I mean not a real he-man. Slightly built, shall we say? Now how do we get at this? Well, maybe there is an element of guessing here, Tony. It's just that he has never attempted anything that requires great physical strength. He didn't dig deep holes for the bodies.' Tony looked sick. 'Yes, there are bodies. But not bruised. Treated gently, we think. Not a rough killer. Did you say something? I thought you made a comment.'

'He didn't say anything,' said Dove. He was sitting with his arms folded, staring at Tony Young. He looked grim and sombre: this was his professional look.

'One other thing about this person (and it fits in with him being local) is that we are sure the girls all knew him. He was someone in their lives. Either they knew him directly or they knew his mother or his sister or his wife.'

'Do you think so?' said Tony. He had pulled himself together a little and seemed steadier.

'Yes. They trusted him, you see, Tony,' said Coffin softly. 'They must have done. He was a friend. Perhaps a friend of the family.'

'That's rotten,' said Tony. He was definitely more confident now.

'All these girls were girls who wanted a bit of affection. Nice kids, but ones that felt they had some love coming to them. This made them vulnerable.'

'I reckon it was the same for him too,' said Tony. 'You've got to see his way too.'

'Is that an admission of knowledge?'

'You know it isn't,' said Tony defiantly. 'At first, when

175

you started, I thought well perhaps it will be me he's drawing a picture of, but as you went on I knew it wasn't.'

'It has a lot of you in it.'

'The way you arranged it, it has. But I could do it for you, too. You live round here, you could be trusted, maybe you knew the girls and perhaps you aren't all you seem. Question and answer, that's what you were treating me to. It's a treatment.'

'Don't get so noisy.'

'I'm not noisy,' said Tony. He had been shouting. 'I'm defending myself.'

There was a knock at the door. Joan Eames poked her head round the door. She looked bright-eyed and rested. 'I've got her here,' she said. 'Do you want her in?'

Coffin nodded.

Joan opened the door wider, beckoned and a small figure wearing a bright summer dress and white shoes came in.

'Good morning, Kim,' said Coffin.

Kim flicked him a bright professional smile. 'Here I am,' she said. 'You said you wanted me. What do you want? Mum's outside.'

'Oh, she'd better come in,' said Coffin quickly. The Simpson family struck him as skilled barrack-room lawyers who might easily bring trouble to a poor policeman. He went to the door himself. 'Come in, Mrs Simpson.'

'I'd like a seat if it's not too much trouble,' said Mrs Simpson, looking round in a hostile way at the room full of men. Parr pushed forward a chair and Tony Young stood up nervously, as if now she was sitting he must stand. Kim's eyes flicked at him. She smiled.

'A friend of yours?' said Coffin.

'Yes, sure. Hello, Tone.'

'Hello.' There was no doubt about his nervousness now.

'Tony's not quite in your age group, so you don't play together,' began Coffin.

'Here!' said Tony.

Kim looked enigmatic. It occurred to Coffin that she would be terrifying by the time she was twenty. If she lived that long.

'But has he ever invited you to go anywhere with him?' Mrs Simpson made a movement. 'No, don't interrupt, Mrs Simpson.'

'Oh well,' said Kim. She had enormously long eyelashes and she let them fall on her cheek. 'Well, sort of.'

'Everyone knows she's the biggest little liar in the business,' said Tony dispassionately.

'Oh,' Kim opened her eyes wide. 'You know what I mean, Tone, you said come and have a walk and meet me at the swings.'

'I was *joking*.'

'Yes, it was true you never came.' She too could be detached.

'Anyway, it was years ago. When you were a little kid.'

'Nothing since?' said Coffin, watching Kim.

'My Kim'd never do anything wrong,' said Mrs Simpson.

'No, of course not. But she did go missing for a little bit, didn't she? You reported her missing.'

'But that was all a mistake. Kim came back. She wasn't missing. But we have to take special care.'

'Yes, she came back. But we never really got to the bottom of that, did we?'

'We did.' She was flushed and indignant. But Kim was calm.

'Don't be so protective, Mrs Simpson. You may be

covering up more than you know.' He turned to Kim Simpson. 'Tell me the truth, Kim, about that afternoon. Where did you go? And with whom?'

She seemed to appreciate the accuracy of his grammar. 'With whom,' she repeated questioningly to herself. She took a deep breath. 'I was not with whom anyone.'

'Oh, Kim.'

'Well, I wasn't with him, at all events,' said Kim, looking at Tony Young. 'Why, I never would.'

'Thanks,' said Tony. 'And I mean that.'

Kim gave a pleased wriggle as if she had somehow scored. 'Oh, Tone,' she said.

I bet I could get something out of you if I had you alone, thought Coffin. A certain frail delicacy about her struck him. She had blue shadows under her eyes. She looked full of vigour, but somehow not strong. Coffin had a child himself and knew the difference between the look of perfect health and this.

He looked at Parr and gave a slight nod. Parr rose, tapped Tony Young on his shoulder and got him out of the room. Coffin knew they were going to the small questioning room just down the corridor and that there Tony would be taken through question and answer again. Or perhaps even just left to think.

When they had gone, he said, 'Could I have a word with you on your own, Mrs Simpson?' He didn't have to look at Joan Eames; she had already drawn Kim to the window and was talking to her in a friendly way. She was a good policewoman.

'Yes?' said Kim's mother suspiciously. She turned her head slightly.

'Your daughter's all right,' he said, following her gaze to where it rested on Kim at the window.

'You're anxious about her, aren't you?' he added.

'Oh well,' she was evasive, willing to shrug off the question.

'There's something you haven't told me about her, isn't there, Mrs Simpson?' Behind him he could hear Kim chattering away to Joan Eames; heard but not seen she seemed much more childlike. That air of sophistication was illusory, learnt, put on, not really understood by the wearer.

'I'm strict with her.'

'Yes, I'd noticed that.'

'I love my Kim,' she said defensively.

'Of course you do.' All the same, he thought with mounting excitement, there's something that puts her in the same category as the others. She's one of them.

'Is it her health?'

'Oh, we don't talk about that,' she said at once.

'Still, if there is something, I'd like to know. Perhaps I ought to know.'

'Well, poor child, we don't tell her the name of it. Just take doctor's pills, we say. We don't want her to feel different.'

She does feel different though, Coffin thought.

'You have to watch her, that's all. You have to see she doesn't take too much sugar.'

'She's diabetic?' said Coffin.

'Yes,' said Mrs Simpson in a low voice. 'She won't grow out of it. She's not bad, but you have to watch her. Not let her get at the sweet things too much. No sweets, no ice-cream I have to say to her sometimes. She loves ice-cream. Of course, if everything's properly balanced it's all right, the doctor says. But we don't say anything to Kim. You can't explain to a child, can you?'

Coffin glanced across to the window. 'She seems a

pretty intelligent child to me. I should think you could tell her.'

'Oh, I'd rather she just thought her old mum and dad were grumpy.'

Coffin felt rather sad. 'Are you right?'

'I want her to think she's absolutely perfect,' said Mrs Simpson. She held her head high.

Kim turned from the window and faced her mother. Coffin, seeing her gaze, half wise, half perplexed, knew that not only had her mother failed to protect her perfection but had infected the child with a terrible doubt. The doubt was growing with her and changing her as she grew.

The telephone rang. He picked it up, listened for a moment and then said, 'Wait a minute.' Once again he had only to look at Joan Eames and she knew what to do. She got Kim and her mother comfortably outside the room in a smooth running movement that didn't alarm them. They were smiling as they went as if everything had been their own idea and they'd thought of it themselves.

Only Coffin and Dove were left. Coffin resumed his call. 'Right. Go on now.' He listened and as he listened he made notes on the pad in front of him.

He looked across at Dove. 'The first report on the girls' bodies,' he communicated, and then went back to listening. 'Yes, yes. I get that.'

Dove waited.

'Well, well,' said Coffin and put the receiver down. He looked at Dove. 'We ought to shoot ourselves. We missed something. Something? We must have missed everything.'

Dove still waited, looking cynical and resigned. He brushed off Coffin's words. He wasn't going to shoot himself and he didn't believe he'd missed too much. Maybe there was something slightly understressed but missed, no. He didn't believe it. If they looked it would be there.

'Let's have it then,' he said.

'In the stomach of two of the children roughly the same things were found.' Dove stirred at once. 'No, they hadn't been drugged. Not with poison at any rate. No. There was skim milk, cocoa, colouring, glyceryl monostearate and flavouring – vanilla.'

Dove looked at him. 'Sounds edible.'

'Ice-cream,' said Coffin.

He dropped the words into the silence on the room.

Ice-cream, he had said. Ice-cream. Ice-cream. Ice-cream.

Chapter Seventeen

'Of course we checked on the ice-cream van,' said Dove.
'The Parker child disappeared from Belview Street which
is the other side of the Liddell and House factory. Here,
you can see.' He pointed to the map. 'We asked in all the
network of little roads, Pansy Place, Allison Road, Letts
Street, if anyone had seen the ice-cream van. Admittedly
it was a wet night and not many people were out, but no
one had seen it. So we ruled it out. And, of course, we
made other checks too. At the depot where the vans are
housed. I'll tell you about those later.'

'And what about the night Katherine Gable went?'

'Well, we asked around that set of streets too. This
time Harper Street, Archery Road and Peel Terrace. She
went from the other side of the district. No, was all the
answer we got. Not seen. So we accepted his story.'

Now Cy Read was right out in front.

'Read has always been one of the men we suspected, of
course. But we couldn't make any proof he was ever on
the scene.'

'Well, obviously we're going to have to look harder.
The ice-cream the children ate means something. It has
to.'

'Yes, I suppose so,' said Dove. There was an unspoken
war between him and the scientific branch of the detective team and he really hated the thought that they had
come up with a contribution that mattered. And yet he
used their services all the time.

'Get hold of Read and start talking to him. Get him talking.'

'And Tony Young?'

'Keep him here too. I haven't finished with him.'

Dove got up. 'And the girl, Kim Simpson?'

Coffin thought. 'She can go home. But tell her mother to keep her in the house.' He added. 'Let Eames deal with the girl side of it.'

'She's going to enjoy that.'

'She's good at it, though.'

There was an air of intense activity over the whole place now.

Joan Eames led Mrs Simpson and Kim home. She thought they were both silent. They said that they would walk home alone and wouldn't take a ride and anyway would prefer to be on their own. All the same, Joan insisted on walking with them. No one spoke much on the short trip.

'Stay home now,' said Joan Eames.

'Yes.' Mrs Simpson nodded. She meant as much by this as anyone usually did. She'd stay home, yes, but if she had to got out to shop then she'd go out to shop. But she would regard that as staying at home.

Then Joan Eames returned to the small office she shared with two other people. Kim and Mrs Simpson had been sitting in it while they waited. She opened a window and tidied her desk. An ashtray had to be emptied where Mrs Simpson had been smoking. Joan herself did not smoke. Kim had fidgeted round the room, not really sitting anywhere. She had spent most of the time staring out of the window.

'I suppose the poor kid does quite a bit of that one way and another,' thought Joan Eames. Without having over-heard the conversation between Coffin and Kim's mother, she had yet grasped that somehow Kim was a prisoner. Kim seemed to have amused herself tearing up paper. Neatly Joan tidied it away.

She had taken no part in the investigation of Cyrus Read and for quite some time no one told her the exact details of what had been discovered about the children, although, of course, rumours were soon flying round.

Coffin was studying a street map of the district. It was large scale and marked with red circles to indicate where the missing girls had last been seen. There seemed no sort of pattern in these places, except that they were all near each other and near Saxe-Coburg Street.

They certainly didn't relate to the route of the ice-cream van. There was no indication it had been seen at those places at those times.

All the same Coffin was a local boy, had grown up round here, and an uneasy question was struggling to the surface of his mind. As a child he had played in streets like these children and he thought it ought to help him to an idea.

Wasn't there a game they had played around those streets, hide-and-seek? Catch-as-catch-can? But children always played these games. He and Dove went over the problem again and again, each time getting nowhere. It seemed to be a moment for action, but all they could do was to walk ground where they had been before.

'All along we had our eye on Read,' said Dove. 'But especially after the last child but one, Katherine Gable, went missing. You know we did.'

'I remember that,' said Coffin. 'I remember we had him in. I didn't question him myself. You did, didn't you?'

'Yes. We said to him: Are you sure you didn't have

184

your van out that night? And he said no. Not one of his nights for being on evening shift.'

'Checked?'

'Oh yes, it checked out. We asked at the depot. It's a smallish local firm. And they said: no, Cyrus Read was not working on either of those nights. He's a sort of foreman figure and hardly ever does a night shift, although some of those vans keep going until about midnight in the summer. He used to work like that, and it was on one of those night shifts he got interested in UFO sightings. But then he got promotion and doesn't do them any more.'

'And where do they keep the vans when not in use?'

'Locked up in the depot.'

'Checked there?' said Coffin.

'Yes. We asked. It seemed enough at the time.'

Coffin sat thinking for a moment. At the time, as Dove said, a question had seemed enough. Cy Read had only been a possibility, a figure on the outskirts of the crime. Now he was right in the middle.

Coffin got up. 'Let's go. One asking wasn't enough. I want to know more about that van and its movements.'

By now it was warm afternoon.

'Where is Read now?' asked Coffin.

'We took him in on his way to work this morning. He's in cold storage now. Waiting in an interview room. I'd like to leave him for a bit.'

'What's he doing?'

'Walking up and down and talking aloud.'

'What about?'

'Nonsense mostly. Something about a flying saucer.'

'What does he say?'

'He seems worried about them.'

'What about them?'

Dove said cheerfully: 'He's worried about the coincidence of there being a sighting and a girl being missing all at the same time.'

'I'm worried too,' said Coffin grimly. 'It's too good to be true.'

The ice-cream van which Cyrus Read drove operated from a small depot not far away. The manager of the Kandy Kream Ices South London depot greeted them.

'Saw you coming.' He nodded to Dove whom he had met. 'You came before?'

'Yes.'

'And now you've come again,' he said in a slightly hostile tone.

'Just checking.'

'Yes.' The manager's eyes studied them. 'Two of you.' He was a short, plump man with shrewd grey eyes. 'Important matter, eh?'

'Yes, it is,' said Coffin.

'Getting near an arrest, eh? Don't think any of my men can be involved.'

Dove didn't answer directly, instead he said: 'This is Superintendent Coffin. Can we come in and talk?'

'To me?' He sounded surprised.

'To you first. Others later perhaps.'

'Cy hasn't come in today.'

'No.'

Dove didn't make it a comment. Coffin still hadn't spoken.

'I sent a message round to his wife but he isn't there.'

'He'll turn up.'

'Oh quite. That's what I said to her.'

'She wasn't worried?'

'Not till she heard he wasn't here. Not till then. Well, sit down, gentlemen.' He offered them two upright chairs

186

made of chrome and plastic in his crowded office. He didn't have very much in it except a desk and chairs, but it was so small that this still made a crowd. 'I'm quite sure none of my men can be mixed up in you know what. I'm not a fool. I check on my men very carefully before I take them on. I know kids hang around ice-cream vans. I don't employ crazies, Inspector.' He settled himself back in his chair. 'I'm not called Di Finzio for nothing. I've got Italian blood. I'm a good family man. My brother and I have twelve kids between us.'

'Your brother the Di Finzio who runs the fairground?'

'That's right. Doing well. Got six boys away at boarding school. I like mine at home.'

'About your vans,' said Coffin, speaking for the first time.

'What about them?'

'Who looks after them here?'

'There's a chap who services them. He's responsible for checking them in and out.'

'And at night?'

'Well, he lives above the garage, if that's what you mean. He's a sort of night watchman as well.' He turned to Dove. 'You saw him, you spoke to him.'

'It's his turn again,' said Coffin.

'He's a very decent straightforward chap,' said the manager.

'Of course.'

'I wouldn't like him to be under suspicion.'

'What's his name?'

'Joe Coppel.'

'And where is Joe Coppel?'

The manager led the way to the window and pointed. 'That's Joe Coppel.'

Outside in the yard was a van. Kandy Kream, it said on

the side. And from under the van a pair of legs protruded, just about beneath the K in Kream. 'He's working on the left back wheel. Trouble there.'

'Let's go out and speak to Joe Coppel.'

'I wish you'd come right out and say what you really mean,' said the manager, watching them go.

Joe Coppel seemed quite glad to crawl out from under the K in Kream. 'Hot there,' he said, wiping his hands on a piece of rag. He nodded to Dove. 'Back here again?'

'A few more questions about these vans. We've seen the time-table and the work-sheets. How they come out and how they come in. Who works what hours, but there are other things. You drive, I suppose.'

'I can drive, of course,' said Joe Coppel. 'I've never actually taken one of these for a joy-ride, if that's what you mean. Bit conspicuous it would be for my girl friend.'

'Are you sure these vans are always locked up each night?'

'I'm the only one with a key.'

'Perhaps we ought to check you too.'

'You can if you like. I thought you were doing so.'

'Isn't there ever a night when all the vans don't come home? What happens in an emergency?'

'We've never had one.'

'When do you go off duty?'

''Bout six.'

'And supposing one of the vans is late? What happens? Do you wait?'

'They're never late.'

'But there might be a breakdown? Can't they 'phone through and tell you?'

'Never have.'

'Are you telling me that all the vans are always here every night?'

'Late-night drivers park them in summer outside their own homes. They get special permission for that. But that don't apply to what you're asking about.'

'And what about Cyrus Read. Are you sure he never takes his van home late?'

'He's a foreman.'

'So?'

'Well, once or twice he has 'phoned up to say he wouldn't be bringing it in. Only nights he was in a hurry.'

Coffin leaned back in triumph. He looked at Dove and they knew they had some questions to ask Cyrus Read.

'Yes,' said Cy reluctantly. 'Some nights if I was busy I didn't take the van in.'

'Where was it?'

'I parked it near home.'

'Where?'

'Couple of places. Mostly back of John Plowman's shop. He's got an open yard there. It made an easier journey home for me. Practically nothing. It was safe enough. I locked it.'

'And you kept the key?'

'Yes.' He moved uneasily. 'What's the harm? Why the questions?'

'And on what dates did you leave the van in this way?'

'I can't name dates that way.'

'Try.'

Cy moved restlessly. 'It didn't happen more than half a dozen times. Nights I had a special meeting or there was a UFO sighting.'

His eyes met Coffin's and then fell. 'Yes,' he said. 'Well, I see how it sounds. I suppose you'd have to call it coincidence.'

'That would be an easy answer. I'm paid to do better than that. I'll talk to you later.'

'You really want it to be me, don't you?' said Cy. He was hustled off to the penitential waiting room again.

It fitted so neatly and they were all so happy it should be Cy. They all disliked him. He seemed to have the basic gift for arousing hostility which seemed necessary for a really popular murderer. Yes, no one would mind if Cyrus Read proved to be the man they wanted. Except perhaps his wife, who was Dave Edmondstone's sister.

'Have we really got him, though?' queried Coffin. 'We've never really pinpointed the ice-cream van in the streets around where a child went.'

'We just have to look a little harder that's all,' said Dove confidently. 'If it was there we shall find someone who saw it. Bound to.'

'Get on with it then.'

'And Read? What about him at the moment?'

'Leave him until you get a witness to the van's appearance.'

Four hours later Dove returned and admitted that, so far, it was defeat. 'We can't find anyone who says they saw an ice-cream van around one of those streets at the time any one of the kids went.'

'Are you asking in the right places?'

'We're asking in the streets where they went from,' said Dove tersely. 'But it doesn't mean anything. They're deaf and blind round here, that's all.'

'Dumb too?' asked Coffin. 'No, it means something all right. I think it's time we talked with Read again.'

But now they had him in the room again, Cy Read was quiet, hostile and would not talk. If you didn't like him, and hardly anyone did seem to like Cy these days, you could call him sulky. It was amazing, the swift run downhill into dislike that Cy had known. He could remember the time when he had been a respected, looked-up-to man in good standing. A family man with credit. But he had felt his rating drop slowly and mysteriously over the months until now when the police had come for him.

It seemed inevitable he should be a suspect, he recognized it was what everything had been building up to, but he resented it. So he wouldn't talk.

Coffin, looking at him, thought he had to be made to talk. 'I hear you're interested in science.'

There was a pause. 'New science,' said Cy. 'Not that old stuff. New science, that's what it's called.'

'Flying saucers, and so on? I heard you were interested.'

'Everyone knows. It's why they hate me.'

'Do they hate you?' said Coffin with interest.

'Don't trust me, anyway. I'm a working man who doesn't believe in the conventional things they believe in and believes in things they laugh at. You laugh yourself, don't you? Yes, I can see it.'

'I'm not laughing now.'

'Only because you think you're doing something better. You think you've got me. Well, you haven't.'

'No?'

'You'll never get me,' said Cy, with utter conviction in his voice.

'But you admit you had the van out on certain nights.'

'Those were nights I was busy. Nights of meetings of the Club.'

'Also nights when girls disappeared.'

Cy was silent. But his jaw set obstinately and Coffin knew that they would never get a confession from him.

So far they had nothing but the ice-cream the children

had eaten to point the way to Cy. Give them time and they would come up with something. Something like a fingerprint or a shred of cloth or a wisp of hair that could be linked with Cy. But time was short. There was still a child missing.

'Tell us where Belle Anderson is and I'll make it easy for you,' Coffin said.

Cy was silent.

'God, I can remember when I was a happy man,' said Cy. 'Not since I came here, though.'

'That's right, Cy,' said Coffin, suddenly remembering. 'You don't come from round here, do you?'

'I wasn't born in the sacred precincts, if that's what you mean. Moved here so my wife could be near her mother. She died six years ago, left us the boy, and we're still here.'

'You don't belong here but your wife does.'

'Yes, that's how they put it round here. Feels that way too.' He gave Coffin a sour look. 'You're one of them. You *think* like them.'

'I'm trying to,' said Coffin. 'I'm trying really hard to think like someone who lives round here because I think that's the way to get the answer I want.'

Cy bared his teeth in a cross smile which wasn't meant to show humour, and didn't – just resentment. 'Childhood games,' he said.

Because beneath the surface of his mind deep movements had been carrying buried memories upwards without his realizing it, it was a shock to Coffin when he suddenly found himself remembering one childhood game. But the shock was also that he should have forgotten. Somehow the psychologists would say he must have wanted to forget.

He could even recall the girl's name, Tissie. She

couldn't have been christened Tissie, but that was how he remembered her; Tissie Martin. They had been playing a game of hide and seek, and his motives in choosing hide and seek had not been entirely above suspicion nor hers in joining in. Looking back, perhaps it hadn't been the first doubt he'd had, he'd had double feelings about the episode all these years. Because his response to Tissie's uninhibited version of a children's game had been vivid and physical to his alarm and delight.

He looked at Cy. There but for the grace of God, he thought, and then, no. No. Everyone's behaviour sprang from common impulses, but it didn't have to end in murder. And with the normal person, it didn't.

Tissie Martin and Liddell and House, the shoe polish factory. It had been a slightly derelict affair even in those days and it was in their yard that he and Tissie had played stimulating games.

He looked at the map that hung on the wall. Liddell and House lay between Belview Street and Peel Terrace. It fronted one and backed on the other. You could back a van in one set of doors and come out with it through another. He should have remembered before.

'The Liddell and House factory is empty, isn't it?' he said aloud.

'Yes,' said Cy. 'It's going. All that land is due to be cleared.'

'Not even a watchman around?'

'I don't know.'

'Oh, come on, you know. That's the sort of thing you know. You know you could back your van in that derelict yard and never have it seen. You could be near Belview Street when Grace Parker went and never be noticed. You could be around Peel Terrace and never be seen there either.'

'You prove that,' said Cy, and gave the ghost of a laugh.

'I might be able to do that. All three children had been eating ice-cream.'

'As far as I'm concerned it's all imaginary. It didn't happen.' His voice gathered strength. 'All you've got is a bit of vanilla. You can't keep me here because of a trace of ice-cream.'

He spoke with a kind of desperate cockiness.

'You can't make me say anything I don't believe,' he said. The lines in his face became hard and firm.

Coffin understood what he read there. It was faith.

He no longer thought Cy likely to be the murderer. For the first time he saw that of all people in the case, Tony Young, John Plowman, even himself, Cyrus Read was a man of faith. He believed he was in touch with other worlds.

'And do you know why I believe?' said Cy. 'Because I've fought for my scientific achievements. I've had to fight hostility from the orthodox – those who get their education the straight way and go on believing what they're taught. Well, I never was educated because my dear dad said I must get out and earn. So I've taught myself, and I came out the better for it.' He gave Coffin a pale glare, but he wasn't really looking at him, what he was glaring at was his past, in which his father had robbed him of an education, and his future, which was threatened by the conventional-minded. 'I know I'm right: there are minds out there and they're speaking to us.' He threw out his arm. 'How cheap it is that we don't listen.'

There was a moment's silence. 'I'm ahead of my time,' said Cy. 'Born before my time. Now's the time to be born.'

'Where were you born, Read?' asked Coffin.

'Honor Oak. Know where that is?'

'I know,' said Coffin. 'When did you move here?'

'When I married. I married too young. My dad still lives over there. And the reason he couldn't let me get educated,' said Cy, determined to take it back to the previous generation, 'was because he'd got married young. It goes on and on.'

'You fond of children?' asked Coffin suddenly.

'Not specially. And not other people's children.'

This was Coffin's last question. After it, he let Cyrus Read go.

Chapter Eighteen

They had had Tony Young in as a suspect and had to let him go. They had had Cyrus Read in as a prime suspect and had to let him go, too.

Dove was angry. He was looking for someone to blame. Coffin was to hand, but it was difficult to put this into words. He managed to get the feeling across, though.

'I don't trust either of them,' he said. 'They could be in it together.'

'It's an idea. I don't think so, though.' Coffin had his temper in control. But only just. Another few days of this and he and Dove would be in a fight of their own. It had been hanging over them for a long while now, nicely kept in check by the fact that they really liked and respected each other. Perhaps the tender flower of friendship couldn't take deep root in police service but they had a decent relationship. Otherwise Dove was ambitious, unimaginative and sceptical of his superior's longer flights of the imagination. They had worked together for too long now; it was time for a shake-up.

'Your car all right since you got it back?' he asked absently.

'Yes. And I found out about a nice little racket.'

'A new one?'

'An old one with knobs on. A chap called Russell was buying wrecked cars, removing all identification plates; then he was going out and pinching other cars of the same make, switching plates and then making a sale. And then, if you please, he was re-stealing the cars, re-fixing the

plates and leaving the car to find its way home to its
original owner.'

'But leaving the chap in the middle with no car at all?'

'And none to find.'

'That was how your car went?'

'Yes.' Dove looked thoughtful. 'I shall never know who
had my car.'

'I should look for a kid that's crying for a rubber duck,'
said Coffin. They looked at each other.

'Dead end,' said Dove.

'There are certain things we can still do,' said Coffin.

'And I know just what you're going to say,' said Dove,
getting up. 'Routine, routine, routine.'

'Yes, that's one thing. It's the way that pays off in the
end. And the other is, watch Kim Simpson.'

Routine, within minutes, brought them the news that
the children whose bodies had been interred in Slippers'
Old Garage had died through suffocation. They had not
been drugged.

'Except with ice-cream and kisses,' said Coffin with a
groan.

'Kisses?'

'Yes,' he pointed to a sentence in the report.

It read: 'Around the mouth and on the cheeks of Child
A (Katherine Gable?) are small bruises. As there are also
signs of red colouring matter and grease, probably lipstick, these marks may be kisses.'

'A woman?' said Dove, incredulous. 'That would
explain a lot.'

'I think we ought to see Kim Simpson again,' said
Coffin, stretching out a hand for the telephone. With a
few words he sent Joan Eames running.

'There's no woman in this case,' said Dove. 'Not close
in.'

'Aren't there? I see two.'

'A woman alone, do you think? Or two of them working together?' Both Dove and Coffin were thinking aloud.

'Jean Young and Cyrus Read's wife. Friends and neighbours both.'

'Does that mean anything?'

'I'm just filling in the background.'

'Do they say what colour the lipstick is?'

'No. Just red. Probably not easy to tell. So we don't know whether blonde or brunette.'

A quick heavy tread down the passage acquainted him with bad news. That girl's never going to get a husband unless she loses weight, he thought as he saw Joan Eames.

'Kim Simpson's not there and her mother doesn't know where she is,' she said breathlessly. 'The kid just walked out and they didn't know she'd gone.'

'I knew she had something on her mind,' said Coffin bitterly. Joan Eames got the classic reward for all bringers of bad news and his anger bounced on her head.

'Go out and do something about it.' Joan flushed and started to move. 'No, wait.' He was still irritable. 'Think about it first.'

'I am thinking about it,' said Joan. She went out and very slightly banged the door.

Dove laughed, not nicely. A quarrel was very near the surface.

With a deliberate gesture, Coffin put out an arm and shoved everything on one side of his desk to the ground, clearing a space. So that measure of violence was out of his system and into the world.

On the space that he had cleared, Coffin put the tape recorder. He put on the tape that Tony Young had given him. He played it.

He listened carefully to the thoughts Tony had put on

it. More and more Tony's voice sounded the voice of innocence and his part that of victim.

Unnoticing, guileless victim. And another figure began to walk around. Coffin was surprised how clear and yet how unobtrusive this figure was.

And with the figure he began to see a place. The Liddell and House shoe polish factory. It seemed to keep appearing, through the clouds. He played the tape again, listening to Tony's voice. A voice which tried to sound old and worldly and only achieved enthusiasm. Damn it, he was beginning to like the boy.

Yes, Tony did tell him on the tape one thing he wanted to know about the factory. He picked up the telephone and spoke to Joan Eames.

'No news, I haven't got her yet,' she said in a flurried way, as soon as she heard his voice.

'I'm not worrying about Kim Simpson at the moment. This is something else.'

'Yes?'

'I want you to go round to the Anderson house and get the boy again. His mother can come too. I'll meet you there.'

He was there outside the Anderson house, waiting, when Joan Eames emerged with the boy and his flushed mother. Jean was holding the boy's hand and soothing the woman.

'Now we'll take this as if we were on an ordinary family walk. You bring the boy and I'll walk along beside you. But I'm leading the way.'

'Belle?' began Mrs Anderson. But Coffin didn't answer her; perhaps he didn't hear her.

He led the way to the old factory and stopped. 'Liddell 'n' House?' he said to the boy. 'Little house?'

'Little house,' said the boy at once. He smiled and

moved forward briskly, dragging Joan Eames with him. 'Little house. Belle? Isobel?'

Coffin patted him on the head. 'Clever boy,' he said absently. His eyes met Joan's over the boy's head. 'Take him home.'

He pushed against the battered old wooden doors which marked the entrance to the Liddell and House factory. Locked, of course. The doors would have to be forced.

But set in the big double doors was a smaller door and this, when he pushed it, swung open.

He watched Joan Eames lead the other two away before he walked in. He walked inside. He found himself in the cobbled passage with the high stone roof where the vans had waited for loading. Here he had played in the old days. He remembered it. Leading off it were a few small rooms and then the factory proper. 'Great old barn of a place,' hadn't one woman worker called it? No one worked there now, and hadn't for years.

He went back to the door and looked out. On either hand were tall protective walls blocking the view of the houses beyond. Yes, if you took a risk you could come and go in here and not be seen. It would be a risk, but this murderer seemed to have had good luck.

He looked at the lock on the big door and thought that although the door was dirty the lock looked clean, cleaner perhaps than it should.

There was an oil stain on the cobbles just behind the door as if a van had stood there and leaked oil.

Everything was very quiet, only his footsteps echoing under the vaulted roof. It was like being in a church. Or a tomb.

In front of him was a door which led to what had been, as he remembered, a small office. He pushed it open.

The room was pretty much as he remembered it in shape and size. You could even see that it had once been an office. But even as he looked around he knew the room had been used recently.

There was a deal table and a couple of chairs. In a corner was a camp bed which might have been for the use of a night watchman. Surely there had been one here for a time? An old screen stood in one corner. Pipes suggested there was a wash-basin behind it.

He walked round the room. Yes, this room had been used. Everything here would have to be tested for prints.

He pushed aside the screen. Then he stopped and knelt down. There was a small bundle trussed up in white sheeting like an Egyptian mummy. From the bundle came a sickly smell.

Coffin had met that smell before. He had no doubt he had found Belle Anderson.

Everything was very quiet, but it seemed to him that all around he could hear the sound of children's feet running.

He lifted up the bundle and the head lolled out, the pale complexion dead white tinged with green, and the mouth broadly splashed with lipstick.

The tape from Tony Young was running again. He let it play. It was time to let Tony start talking.

Chapter Nineteen

Tony, at Last

You couldn't stop me talking. Limbo is the place they put you before you are really quite dead, when you've still got links with this world. You have to wait out your time there, till you know if you are going to be really dead or hang around as a ghost. This was where I had been ever since I last talked to the police. They didn't put me there. I did that myself. I suppose as a sort of punishment to myself for being a fool.

Well, I look like being a restless corpse. I'm coming back to life. And I have plenty to say.

Tony, I said to myself, not only have you got to defend yourself, you have got to be seen to defend yourself. You owe that to your own dignity. I was back on my dignity. You can see how I'd recovered. I owed a lot to Judith.

I knew about the discovery of Belle Anderson within minutes, probably, of it happening. That is definitely not the sort of news you can hide around here. Also, about Kim Simpson. I knew about the other girls, and the ice-cream and pretty well all there was to know. And I knew it left Cyrus Read and me jostling for the hot spot. As we always had been, of course.

And I knew something I thought the police didn't know yet. One of my earliest jobs, when I was still seeking to establish myself in the world, was as night watchman at Liddell and House. It had definite possibilities, that job. It was also the job that first made my sister Jean come half way to giving up her struggle over me. She really thought it was stupid. She didn't entirely give up the struggle, though, and in fact she hasn't given it up now. I was only there two weeks. Enough to get the key and leave plenty of fingerprints around everywhere. I was mad about that.

I still had the key. And I have no doubt at all that Jean knew that I had that key. Her face was looking very peaky these days. She was standing the strain worse than me. If she ever does get to marry that policeman, I'm afraid her responsibilities towards me will prove a serious barrier to a happy married life. I ought to hope that she doesn't marry the policeman. To begin with there's Dad, whom we all tend to forget. Dad, even though a little withdrawn and hardly an ideal parent, has a right not to have to share his house with a copper. But I can't evil-wish Jean. I want things to go right for her.

There's something you have to learn about me and my sister Jean. We are twin souls. Real twins have shared a common birth. I look younger than my years, retarded, you might say, and Jean looks older. She's always had the responsibility of me, you see.

When I started talking and John Coffin suggested I put it on the tape again, I supposed he thought he'd be getting a confession. I'm sure that snarly one, Dove, thought so. And fat girl Eames. But I mustn't let my tongue run away with me. After all, I'm the hero of this story, aren't I? And I have to act like a hero and keep my dignity.

Let me recapitulate what was worrying me: the girl children had all disappeared on nights when both Cyrus and I, owing to the society (now in abeyance) to which we both belonged, seemed to be out on our own. Opportunity for us, in other words.

Then all the children had been taught by my sister Jean and were known to me. They were all friends of Cy's children. Oh yes, I know that. And John Coffin told me it was one of the things he was careful to have Joan Eames establish. So that meant we had a contact. Those kids could have trusted us.

Cy, in addition, had the ice-cream van. But I knew what they thought. I too might have had the ice-cream van. I knew, as well as he did, where he had it parked; round the back of John Plowman's shop.

'You'll get no confession out of me,' I said to Coffin when he brought my tape back, saying he'd got all he could from it and suggesting I start adding to it. Supposing, of course, that was what he meant.

'No,' he agreed. He had me in his office there talking to me, but once again he let me go. I was surprised about that. *Now* I think he was watching to see what I'd do.

It's funny, but you always think of the police as being a sort of machine and feeding in the right questions and getting out the right answers. I suppose there is an element of that too, but they're men as well and sometimes what they put into the machine are more hopes and guesses, and then the answers don't come out right. And even when they've got the right answer, and know it, like *now*, they have to prove it. I think Coffin was worried this was going to be one of the cases where they knew but couldn't get a man to court. He let me go around to see if I'd pull the house down.

I wonder how he knew I had that pull in me? But I suppose that's what makes a good policeman: they can tell things about a person he hardly knows himself.

When Judith, that's my girl friend you may remember, gets to a bit in a play where she can't remember lines she says impatiently that she just ad libs. This must be just in rehearsal. I can't believe that beautiful and skilful though

Judith is they let her write her plays as well as act them. I'm getting to the part where I can't remember my lines so I'll ad lib. Not everything that gets said on the tape from now on really got said, not all the dialogue was as told. But what you hear is what really happened, because that is what remains with me. And that, in the end, *is* the truth.

After seeing Coffin that morning I went round to the shop. It was shut and my boss John Plowman not there. I wasn't too surprised. I'd seen it coming. He's been restless lately. I thought I could probably get in round the back, but I didn't try. I wasn't interested in working that day.

There was a policeman right behind me. 'Well, so you're following me,' I said. He didn't deny it.

I gave the door of the shop a little rattle just for show, and then went on.

I knew where I was going. Perhaps he knew where I was going. I dare say he did. We had the same facts to be drawn upon.

These were the facts: the times the children went, the people they knew, those that they trusted.

The trouble was that nearly all of us in this district had two lives. We were poor, you see. We didn't have the resources to maintain consistency all through our lives. It takes money to do that. So I am both businessman and errand boy. Cyrus is an ice-cream salesman and a scientist in the evening. John Plowman is a shop-keeper and a seer. We're all two-faced round here.

I set off to walk. It may have looked as if I was just taking a desultory path through the streets. But I knew where I was going.

I called on John Plowman's wife. I wasn't sure if I should find her at home. She too had a day-time job. As a nurse, I believe. But she was in, and opened the door herself.

'John in?' I knew he wasn't, of course.

She shook her head. She didn't seem pleased to see me. And I could see signs of packing in the hall behind her.

'I'd like to have seen him.' Not true, of course. I was only probing.

'He's gone. I don't know what we'll be doing about the shop. Or the Club. You'll have to find another job.'

'I wasn't planning on going back to it. He's gone for good then?'

She crossed herself. It was a hangover from a previous life of hers; I don't think she was any longer a believer. 'Yes. Gone for good. I've seen it coming.'

'He's not *dead*, is he?'

She shrugged. 'He might have chosen what you call death. Yes, that might be the vehicle he chose to use.'

I liked that bit about 'what you call death'. She made it sound quite dignified too. 'He did have a choice then?' I said thoughtfully.

'Of course. He told me it might be happening. He couldn't give me an exact date, of course, one never can. But I knew it would be soon.'

'I'd like to have said goodbye.'

'I'm sure he'll get a message through to you if he can,' she said kindly.

I didn't suppose he'd get a message through about the ice-cream van though, and that was what I wanted. In whatever after life he was now engaged in, John Plowman wasn't going to answer questions about that van. I turned away.

Knowing this district like I did, I knew everybody's habits. I knew that Charley Di Finzio would be just going

206

into his brother-in-law's café to have a second breakfast. He was not off his food just because Tom's body and several others had been discovered in premises he had bought up for development. He might be worrying about his investment, but he wouldn't be worried about the bodies. He didn't believe in death. I know he thought he was immortal. He knew other people got it, of course, but he thought that he personally had thrown it off. 'I didn't die in the war, boy,' he said to me once. 'I won't go now.' Frankly, I thought he *had* died during the war and what came back wasn't what had gone into it.

'Where's your asistant, Mr Di Finzio?' I said.

'You want to see him, you can see him,' he said, still chewing his bacon and egg. 'It won't do you any good. You won't get any good out of him. I can't get any good out of him. You did me a bad turn there.'

'Sorry, Charley.'

'He just sits there, you know.'

'I'm sorry. I thought it would work out.'

'You don't think at all, Tony, that's your trouble. And don't call me Charley.'

I did think, but I admit I hadn't been thinking about him particularly.

'Nice boy and all that,' said Di Finzio, still eating, 'but no good as a worker. Just sits. I let you kids play around my fairground. I employ you even. And what do I get for it? Nothing. He does nothing.'

'I'll go on round.'

'In the office,' he said, nodding across the road to the two-room office he had rented when he went into the property business. He was our local tycoon. I had been studying his career to pick up points. I hadn't learnt much though. His career and mine were not going to follow a similar pattern.

I went across the road to the office. There was an outer room and Di Finzio's small inner room. The assistant used the outer office. As far as I remember he wasn't meant to be in much. Assistant to Mr Di Finzio meant messenger boy, really.

The assistant was rummaging round in a cupboard with his back to the door.

'Hello,' I said. He turned round slowly, as if he didn't want to see me.

'Hello, Dave,' I said.

'Oh, it's you.'

'Yes.' I smiled at him. I suppose it didn't come out too pleasant a smile because he flinched.

'You know what I've come for?'

He didn't answer, but sat down. I saw what his employer meant.

'Get up,' I said promptly. He did get up. 'Well, Dave, this is the end. Where's Kim Simpson?'

'Not here.'

'I know that. But where?'

Once again he didn't answer.

'Look,' I said patiently. 'The police aren't fools. They can count. They can see that you had the right opportunities. Any minute now they are going to realize that the reason the girls always went on the nights there was a sighting was because those were the nights Cy was out. And the nights Cy was out he left his van parked at the back of John Plowman's shop. And you could use it. I suppose you stole his van keys and copied them. Like the keys to the Liddell and House factory when I had them. You got them too, I suppose.'

'I was lonely,' said Dave. 'Tony, you *know* that.'

'Was that enough, Dave?' I asked, 'for all you've done?' But even as I said it, I knew, in a way, it was.

It all went back to when we were fifteen years old. That was the summer when for all we knew of the outside world we might have been on a desert island. Me, Dave, and Butty made three. Not that we paid him much attention either, but he was there on the island with us. The island was created this way: we were the only three boys in our class not going on a school trip to Norway. Various reasons produced the same result for us all. I didn't have any money, Dave didn't have any money, Butty didn't have any money. But behind this different circumstances enmeshed us. In my case my father was going a bust on his birds. In Dave's his mother had just died. (He never knew his father anyway.) I don't know what operated with Butty, perhaps his family just wanted him at home. We were outcasts among our better endowed peers.

I was reading a good deal at the time.

'What's the book?' asked Dave.

I told him.

'Oh, a grown-up book.'

'I'm a grown-up boy,' I said.

'I don't read much myself.' I went on with my reading. 'D'you think I should?'

'Up to you.'

'Could you – ' he paused. 'Instruct me? Help me.'

I looked up. 'Can't you *read*?'

'Not really.'

So I taught him to read. I suppose everyone at school but me had known Dave couldn't read, but I hadn't concentrated on him before. He didn't make an easy reader, but I got him along pretty well in the end.

One day Butty joined the reading class. We read our way through various books, some of which I could stand and others which I couldn't, but I had to bear their tastes in mind. And perhaps I let Butty and Dave into worlds they shouldn't have entered. But for me they would never have heard of Freud, Lawrence, Maldoror.

I tried out too many writers on them. I let them into too many minds, it was a bad thing.

When school closed and the happy boys went off to their foreign land we transferred ourselves to the long grass in the park. I've never been back there a lot. I saw too much of it that summer. Perhaps nothing but good would have come from our relationship but for the heat and the drought and the long grass. We weren't the only animals hiding in the long grass. The dry weather had drawn in lots of other little creatures. We couldn't see them, but they were there.

One morning when we came in a great machine was cutting swathes. A family of little field mice had been uncovered and were scuttling about. The cutter, driven by a park-keeper, one of those we knew, a surly figure, had already killed two. Not much to say about them, but a third, frantic to escape, darted in front of the machine. The driver took a slight swerve to make sure of hitting it.

'He did that on purpose,' said Butty.

'Yeah. A swell fellow,' I said. Where he had passed was a squashed pink heap an inch or two around.

'It was little, soft and dead,' said Dave.

'He ought to be punished,' said Butty (who, no doubt because of his history, always had a strong sense for him levelling up) in a suddenly deep voice.

Dave was silent.

It was his bad luck that we met that park-keeper as he was leaving work. It was his double bad luck that it was a narrow alley behind the cricket pavilion across which we were spread out, although not by design. We had him halted whether we wanted or not.

'Best not to go near him.' I don't know whose voice that was, mine probably, but it was too late. Butty pushed him, Dave kicked him, I stood over him.

The man had the bag that he'd kept his lunch in strung on a strap round his neck. We tore it off him and emptied out the contents, rubbish all of it, and threw it on the roof behind us. Funny about roofs and how they attract you when they are low. I suppose they seem out of touch but aren't really.

We ran off and left him lying there. There was a little trickle of blood from his mouth and I thought I could see the pearly gleam of bone through the hair. We thought he was dead. We went on thinking that for days.

Well, we hadn't killed him and I saw him one day in a pub drinking beer, and he didn't even look sick, but you might say he'd killed us. It had been bad, living through those days when we'd thought he was dead.

'We didn't kill that man, Dave,' I remember saying, glad to get the news across. 'I don't believe we even hurt him much and he isn't going to do anything about it. He just turned away when he saw me and went on eating pork pie.'

'Perhaps he didn't know you.'

'He knew me.'

'Better tell Butty then.'

'I already have done.'

'What did he say?'

'He said: that's over then.'

'That's over then,' repeated Dave reflectively. 'We needn't ever see Butty again then?'

'I don't think he wants to much.'

'We're bound to run into each other, though.'

'Yes. You can't throw off things like that.'

'But you and I'll stay together, Tony?'

'If that's how you want it, Dave.'

And that was how it was: you can't throw things off.

Dave was most the gainer from that episode, if gain is the right word. It wasn't that he liked violence. He didn't like it any more than I did but it wasn't alien to him. He was interested. He wanted to know more. He wanted to know more about it in a certain context. Already he knew more about the man who drove over the field mouse than we did. Much much more.

But Dave isn't really able to live on his own, and although he went off once and took a job in Birmingham, he came back, as I knew he would.

Now he said to me piteously: 'I had to have some affection. But, Tony, why are you talking to me like this?'

'Why do you think? I am angry.'

'Why are you talking to me like this, Tony?' He sounded puzzled.

'Lipstick on my shirt, voices on my tape put there by you: why did you do this to me, Dave?'

'Why Tony! How can you talk to me this way? You were there all the time and you knew how it was.'

'No. Don't.'

'Yes. Tony. Why are you going against me like this? It was us together.'

'No. Don't.'

'Lipstick. It got on you because you were there.' He shook his head. 'You taped the voice yourself, Tony. Don't be that way to me.'

'I'll have you crying soon, Dave, won't I?'

'Has it worked on your mind so you've forgotten?' he said, wide-eyed.

'You hate me, Dave.'

'You're acting as if we weren't partners,' he said almost

in tears. 'As if all I did wasn't on your orders. I'm your slave, Tony. You know I am. You've often said so.'

'You're a liar.'

'You wouldn't let me down, Tony, would you?' he pleaded. 'I've done it all the way you wanted. "For my pleasure, slave", you said.'

'I've underestimated you, David.'

'It was to be an academic exercise, you said.'

'I never used that word,' I said in a level voice. 'And I didn't think you knew it.'

'Your word. Your own word,' said Dave obstinately.

'I'd never use that word of murder and cruelty.'

'Don't talk like that. You're turning against me now.'

'I've never been for you, Dave. What exactly *were* you doing?'

'I was making a collection. *You* know.'

'They were your girl friends, weren't they? The ones I never got to see?' I leaned forward. 'Your baby-girl friends.'

'I admit I chose them,' he protested. 'But you knew. And you *saw* them. Later.'

'You're going to say that, are you?'

'I wasn't going to say anything. *You* started it. *Please*, Tony.'

I certainly had underestimated him. 'How did you choose then?' I asked. 'They were all pretty.'

'The first one, the one before I went away, had a silk scarf. I noticed the silk scarf and saw she was a pretty kid . . . You've never asked me this before.'

'You've never told me before, Dave.'

'But *you* told me.' Once again he sounded bewildered. 'I did it the way you said. Make them feel little women. Dress them up. Make-up. Love them a little: it's what they're looking for. But remember they're only kids. Give them ice-cream.'

'That's a truly appalling picture you're drawing me, Dave,' I said, closing my eyes. 'You're showing me too much.'

'It's real, Tony,' he said in a soft voice. 'Real for us both.'

'No. I deny that. I'll always deny it. And I certainly didn't tell you to kill Butty.'

'Butty? You had a bit of luck there, Tony, if you did but know it. He came into the fairground after me. He didn't like you any better than I do. He said: "Tony Young could be in trouble with the police about a trick he wants to play. Why don't you and I gang up on him?" But I was loyal, Tony. I stayed with you.'

'You hated Butty, just like you hate me,' I said, the surprise all mine this time. 'It goes back to when we were kids. *You* were the one Butty made cry. *You* were the one whose bag he used to throw up on the shed roof.' It was bad to think that murder had come out of that group of boys, but it had.

'I did it all for you,' said David. 'Whatever I've done, you shared it with me.' He fixed his eyes hard on me, protuberant and blue. 'Butty came round to the fairground after he'd tried to pull your little trick for you. We went up to the top of the Big Dipper where I was doing a little repair for Mr Di Finzio and I pushed him right over. Broke every bone in his body. He didn't even scream and no one was there to see.'

'But why did you put the girls' things and Butty's knife where they would be found?'

'That was no hiding-place, it was a *showing* place,' said Dave. He laughed.

'Now you've admitted something,' I said quietly. 'You

don't realize it, but you've shown yourself up. Not me. Not Butty. Just yourself. You demonstrated malice towards Butty by placing his knife together with a few of the girls' possessions in that spot you associated with his humiliation of you.' I could feel the words rolling out of me like an act of condemnation. 'More than that: you demonstrated you had been close to the girls.'

'Perhaps it was a false move,' he said sulkily. 'But there's no need for you to sound off at me like that. I did it for your protection.'

'Nothing to do with me, David.'

'Don't throw me off,' he said. 'You can't say you aren't in it too.'

'You're forgetting something: only *you* used the van to trap the kids and transport their bodies, *and* Butty's. Because you must have done that. How did you get the girls in there? By showing them all the ice-cream and offering a free one? Soon, Dave, the police will be checking that van. You didn't work with that van and leave no trace.'

'But *you* killed them.' He looked at me. 'I shall swear it.'

I knew that once he'd used the word kill his state was hopeless. He was really wicked. Not mad. He knew what he'd been doing because he said 'kill'. He ought to have said something else.

'And my tapes?' I said. 'The stuff you put on them and then took off?'

He smiled. This time it was my turn to be on the receiving end of a smile. But it was enough. I knew how he felt about me and a lot of other things then.

'Thanks,' I said, taking a deep breath. 'Just a joke, eh? I took it quite seriously. To tell the truth, I take the whole thing seriously.'

'Nothing I say to you matters. Nothing I do to you matters. No witnesses.'

'Well, I don't want any witnesses, either.'

'But what I want to say to you, Tony, is that it's all your fault. You don't know what it's like having you around talking. You talk about yourself, Tony. Why didn't you talk about me a little?'

'So it's all just between you and me, is it?' I said. 'Just a duel.'

'When I killed Tom Butt I was really thinking about killing you.'

'You should have tried for me first,' I said, 'instead of taking the easy option. I bet Tom was easier to kill.' But he didn't get angry, which I suppose I was hoping for, but just sat there in the way Charley Di Finzio had complained of and let a foul comment drop out as it occurred to him.

'They beat me, you know,' he said. 'Cy beat me when I was quite old. He shouldn't have done that.'

'You've got even,' I said.

'Yes, I've done that.' He contemplated his achievements. Then he said, almost shyly, 'The reason I put things on your tape was that I wanted you to know. I wanted you to be part of it.'

'You're a monster, Dave,' I said.

'And you're so human?'

'Where's Kim Simpson?'

'I sent her home.'

'I don't believe that, Dave.'

'I'm not insatiable.'

'You shouldn't have said that, Dave. It's in very bad taste. Where is she?'

'She surely isn't here.'

'You've got a place, Dave, another place; I'm sure of it.'

I thought of the fairground. There were plenty of hiding places among the booths and tents. In particular I remembered one caravan.

I looked at him speculatively. He was still sitting there, big and sprawling. I've never been a violent boy but I felt violent then.

'You touch me and I'll bash you,' he said.

'The caravan at the fairground, is that it, Dave boy?' I said. Naturally he didn't answer; I hadn't expected him to get up and bow and say yes. 'Tell me, boy. No? You think you're stronger than me? Well, there's something you don't know about me.' I leaned forward across the desk where he was sitting. He put his arm up to ward me off and I got it in my grip. He tried to get up but I pushed him back, using his own arm as a pressure point. 'While you were away I took a course in judo. I wasn't very good, but I learnt one or two tricks.'

He tried to move and I twisted his arm. 'Caravan, Dave? Tell me. I could break your arm,' I said softly. I could break my own too; he had muscles like iron, but naturally I didn't say so.

'You persuade the kids to go to your hidey-holes, feed 'em up with ice-cream and then kill them. We won't go into any embroideries. Did they all think you were their big brother?' I was just going on talking to pass the time; I was hurting him and I fancied to go on hurting him.

His face had gone red and lines had appeared around his mouth and eyes. I suppose this was the face of him the girls saw at the last.

Then with all his strength he pushed against the desk, forcing me backwards. Then he stood up. 'I'll say you're guilty with me till the minute I die,' he shouted.

I had dropped his arm, but I knew I couldn't stand still. So, without conscious thought, reverting to a child-like defence, I pushed him hard with both hands in his chest. It was the sort of thing I might have done to him as a lad of twelve.

His foot slipped, he went back, and his head cracked against Mr Di Finzio's steel filing cabinet. He lay on the floor without moving. A little trickle of blood appeared at one nostril. I thought he looked as dead as anyone could be.

'What I've done for you, Kim Simpson,' I said aloud.

There she was sitting on the floor of the caravan, licking an ice-cream. She looked at me with great terrified provocative eyes.

'Get out of here.' I held open the door. She didn't move except to give a coquettish little flirt of her eye-lashes. 'Get out of here and home to mother before I belt you,' I said harshly.

'No. Why should I?'

'This is why,' and I raised my hand. You knew straight away that violence was the only thing for her. In that I agreed with Dave. 'You don't know what's good for you.'

I pulled her to her feet, she let herself go limp. 'Stiffen up,' I said. 'And move.'

She did move then. What she said as she pushed past me was more terrible to me than anything I had heard from Dave. From now on I believe in the absolute corruptibility of the human mind.

'You fool,' she said. 'I could have made him pay.'

I watched her running home. I didn't see much of a future for her.

I was trembling as I walked home.

* * *

I came back here and I am talking on to my tape. I have telephoned the police to tell them what I did and now I'm sitting waiting. I hope they'll believe me.

From where I sit by the window I can see the one called Dove getting out of the car. John Coffin is behind him. I saw Dove hesitate for a moment at the kid next door who is *still* yelling for his rubber duck, and then come on.

I thought that if I came through this whole (even if I had killed Dave) and had a life again then I'd marry Judith. Anyway, someone has to look after that white car of hers.

Dove rang the door bell.

As I rose to answer it, my eyes fell on the sky, which was darkening into night. I saw a bright light blink there. It moved, then blinked again. Perhaps old John Plowman was up there sending me a signal. Maybe a space ship had stopped by and picked him up, and maybe one day he would be back. Who could tell?

The light winked once more. It didn't look like a star. I'll think about it later. Perhaps I don't have to worry too much about my problems here on this earth. Perhaps there is another solution.

COLLINS CRIME

The Night the Gods Smiled
Eric Wright

A Charlie Salter Mystery

'Good Canadian background, interesting hero, deft plotting and good writing: it all adds up to a sparkling debut.' T. J. Binyon, *The Times Literary Supplement*

The night the gods smiled on Toronto professor David Summers he was murdered in a hotel room in Montreal. What was the phenomenal luck which had so elated him earlier than evening, only to vanish like fairy gold? Was it the reason he died?

As Inspector Charlie Salter painfully pieces together the answers he is drawn into a bizarre network of human relationships. There are Summers's colleagues at the conference, each of whom, it seems, has motive for murder. There is his favourite student, the intriguing Molly, and Joyce, his impassive-looking wife, who could both be withholding useful information.

But as the investigation proceeds Salter becomes aware of astonishing parallels between himself and the dead man, and in the end it is these similarities that provide the vital clue to Summers's death.

'Fascinating characters . . . a real find' *Scotsman*

'High competence, high promise' *Listener*

'Suspenseful and convincing'
Christopher Wordsworth, *Observer*

COLLINS CRIME

Even in the Best Families
Rex Stout

A Nero Wolfe Mystery

Private Eye Nero Wolfe had had several sharp but long-distance encounters in the past with powerful mystery man of crime Arnold Zeck. That Zeck was a blackmailer was obvious. That he was perhaps the most potent and utterly ruthless of all underworld characters seemed more than possible. At any rate Wolfe had once told Archie that if he ever had to come to grips with Zeck he would disappear first, so as not to endanger Archie, his orchids, or his old brownstone in lower Manhattan.

Nero Wolfe was a man of his word. When the day arrived that Zeck interfered in his investigations just once more than was good for business Wolfe quietly vanished. The final conflict had begun.

COLLINS CRIME

The Marshal and the Murderer
Magdalen Nabb

The young woman had come to report that her friend was missing. They were both Swiss, teachers; they had come to Florence to learn Italian and stayed on, working illegally. The missing girl had worked as a potter in a small local town and when the Marshal instigated a search there it wasn't long before they found her body.

His inquiries met with suspicion, even hostility, in the inbred, yet deeply divided community with its long memories. Then there were the mysterious wartime tragedies he could get no one to talk about.

Only as the startling truth about the two Swiss girls emerges, intertwining strangely with the bitterness of the past, does the Marshal begin to tie up the ends.

'Hats off once more to strong, cogent Queen Nabb'
Observer

'Bull's eye again! . . . mastery and strength until the last page' Georges Simenon

'Crafted with care. A pleasure to read' *The Times*

Fontana Paperbacks
Fiction

Fontana is a leading paperback publisher of both non-fiction, popular and academic, and fiction. Below are some recent fiction titles.

☐ FIRST LADY Erin Pizzey £3.95
☐ A WOMAN INVOLVED John Gordon Davis £3.95
☐ COLD NEW DAWN Ian St James £3.95
☐ A CLASS APART Susan Lewis £3.95
☐ WEEP NO MORE, MY LADY Mary Higgins Clark £2.95
☐ COP OUT R.W. Jones £2.95
☐ WOLF'S HEAD J.K. Mayo £2.95
☐ GARDEN OF SHADOWS Virginia Andrews £3.50
☐ WINGS OF THE WIND Ronald Hardy £3.50
☐ SWEET SONGBIRD Teresa Crane £3.95
☐ EMMERDALE FARM BOOK 23 James Ferguson £2.95
☐ ARMADA Charles Gidley £3.95

You can buy Fontana paperbacks at your local bookshop or newsagent. Or you can order them from Fontana Paperbacks, Cash Sales Department, Box 29, Douglas, Isle of Man. Please send a cheque, postal or money order (not currency) worth the purchase price plus 22p per book for postage (maximum postage required is £3.00 for orders within the UK).

NAME (Block letters) _____

ADDRESS _____

_____

_____